Love the Way You Lie

Skye Warren

The woods are lovely, dark and deep,
But I have promises to keep,
And miles to go before I sleep,
And miles to go before I sleep.

—Robert Frost

CHAPTER ONE

I USED TO think there were things I'd never do. Never take my clothes off for money. Never sell my body. Never fuck a stranger just to survive. I'd never sink that low.

I'd rather die.

But it's hard to die, to lie down and let it happen. Not to fight. Not to reach toward the surface for air when you're drowning. It's almost impossible. I'm proof of that. I'm a living example of how low a person would go, if they have to. If they're desperate enough.

If they're staring at the black barrel of a gun, counting their breaths.

I hold my breath as I sweep red across my lips, stark against powder-pale skin. My eyes are already finished with heavy gold liner and shimmery shadow. A stranger blinks at me from the mirror, her eyes wide. She doesn't look sad. Or lonely. She doesn't look terrified, so the makeup's done its job.

On a Wednesday night, the changing room is empty. Even half-priced appetizers can't keep the club full in the middle of the week. No one would dance tonight unless they had to. That's why I'm here. Because I have to be.

Like Candy, who's onstage. And Lola, working the floor. We're doing what we have to do. We're counting our breaths.

I stand and shake out my wings, making sure they're still in place, attached to my bra. It only has to last until I strip it off. The song out there is getting louder and faster, and I know it'll be over soon. My turn next. *Lucky me.*

And I am lucky. I know exactly what the alternative is.

I smooth my panties into place, making sure they're covering the important parts. For now. *Panties* is a generous term for the scrap of fabric designed to tear apart when I tug.

I turn—and freeze. My breath leaves me in a whoosh. Blue is standing in the doorway, leaning against the frame. His thick arms bulge, stretching his T-shirt, tattoos covering the skin I can see. He's ex-military, but whatever sense of honor he might have had is long gone. He's still got discipline though. And power and *force.* He's the club's own mercenary.

How long has he been watching me?

I ignore the chill that slides down my spine. I ignore *him* as I walk toward the door. Maybe he'll move and let me pass. Maybe he won't harass me. And maybe pigs will fly. He grabs my arm.

Which is just as well. It's not like I could have gotten past him without shoving him or something. I'm a lot of things, but I'm not suicidal. So I stand there with his hand on my arm, feeling creepy-crawly tingles all up and down my skin. I don't look him in the eye. I don't like seeing the darkness there. Instead I stare past him, into the dark hallway.

"Not even going to say hi?" He smells like smoke and sweat and alcohol. At only eight o'clock in the evening.

I keep my voice steady. "Hi."

"That didn't sound very friendly. You got a problem with me? Did I offend you in some way?"

Jesus, I don't need this. The song's almost over. If I miss my cue... I shiver. I can't miss my cue. The hallway behind him is empty. Not that anyone would help if they saw. Ivan is the owner of the strip club, along with a cadre of other illegal shit in the city. He's gone most of the time, so even though Blue is just a bouncer, he gets free reign. At least he does a decent job of protecting us girls.

Even if he is an asshole.

"I don't have a problem with you," I say.

He pulls me closer until my body is almost flush with his—and still I won't look him in the eye. He doesn't pay for that. No one does. They pay to touch me, to hurt me. To fuck me. They don't pay me to look them in the eye, so I don't.

His mouth is close enough to my ear that I can feel the whiskers when he speaks. "Then why don't you prove it. Show me how friendly you can be."

Gross. "I'm up next."

His hold tightens, and I can already picture the

bruises. When I'm at home, in the shower, I'll wash off the stench of this place, the shame, but I won't be able to wash off the dark shape of his fingers where they press into my skin. He's imprinting himself on me, becoming part of me, and bile rises in my throat.

"I'm up next," I repeat in a whisper.

Even Blue doesn't want to anger the powers that be. I look up in time to see regret flicker in his eyes. He lets me go. "Later, Honey."

I flinch even though that's my name. Not my real name, but it's what they call me here.

It's who I am here.

When he steps aside, I hurry down the dark hallway. I'm almost more agile in heels than I am barefoot, from all the practice. There are lights on either side of the hallway, track lighting to make the walk feel glamorous or maybe to make sure we don't trip in our stilettos. It feels out of place in the strip club, lighting up what is better dark, dusty corners and ambient shame. It reminds me of a landing strip—not in stripper terminology, but a real airstrip for airplanes with lights on either side to guide me. At any moment I could take off. At any moment, I could be free.

I have to believe that. It's the only way to keep going.

And then I'm backstage, waiting. Trapped. The opposite of free.

I stand behind the curtains. Twenty years ago this area would be filled with stagehands and costume designers and performers waiting for their cue. But now there's just me, shivering in the draft from the air-conditioning as the final strains of music fade away.

Candy slips back, skin shining with sweat and glitter, smelling of booze and cherries. She's the prettiest girl here, except for the track marks on her arms. Except for the black eyes she has too often, ones she skillfully covers with makeup.

The opening notes of my song start playing.

"Depressing," she tells me as she straightens the straps of my bra.

She's never been a fan of my song selection. Apparently, blues is a downer.

"It has a good beat," I say even though she's right. Of course she is. She definitely earns the most of anyone here, and Lola earns more than me too. But if I can't dance classical, I'll at least pick something I want to hear.

She laughs. "A good beat? You still think this is about dancing."

I shake my head, but I'm smiling. She has that effect on people, with her slutty schoolgirl outfit and pigtails. With her bubblegum-pop songs that she strips to. *Branding,* she calls it.

"What's it about then?"

"About fucking, of course." Then she's gone down the hallway, heading toward the dressing room.

My smile falters as I stare after her. What's more depressing than fucking?

I manage to push through the curtain only one beat after my cue. Not that anyone here would notice. Like she said, it's about fucking. About being naked and for sale. Not about dancing. So I drop one foot in front of the other, making my hips pop with each step. A black satin bra. Panties made of black ribbon. It's dark and sexy—and obvious. That's fine with me. I'd rather be forgettable. *I wish I could forget.*

In the first moments onstage, I'm always blinded.

The bright lights, the smoke. The wall of sound that feels almost tangible, as if it's trying to keep me out, push me back, protect me from what's going to happen next. I'm used to the dancing and the catcalls and the reaching, grabbing hands—as much as I can be. But I'm never quite used to this moment, being blinded, feeling small.

I reach for the pole and find it, swinging my body around so the gauzy scrap of fabric flies up, giving the men near the stage a view of my ass. I still can't quite make anything out. There are dark spots in my vision.

The smile's not even a lie, not really. It's a prop, like the four-inch heels and the wings that snap as I drop them to the stage.

Broken.

A few people clap from the back.

Now all that's left is the thin satin fabric. I grip the pole and head into my routine, wrapping around, sliding off, and starting all over again. I lose myself in the physicality of it, going into the zone as if I were running a marathon. This is the best part, reveling in the burn of my muscles, the slide of the metal pole against my skin and the cold, angry rhythm of the song. It's not like ballet, but it's still a routine. Something solid, when very few things in my life are solid.

I finish on the pole and begin to work the stage, moving around so I can collect tips. I can see again, just barely, making out shadowy silhouettes in the chairs.

Not many.

There's a regular on one side. I recognize him. Charlie. He tosses a five-dollar bill on the stage, and I bend down long and slow to pick it up. He gets a wink and a shimmy for his donation. As I'm straightening, I spot another man on the other side of the stage.

His posture is slouched, one leg kicked out, the other under his chair, but somehow I can tell he isn't really relaxed. There's tension in the long lines of his body. There's *power*.

And that makes me nervous.

I spin away and shake my shit for the opposite side of the room, even though there's barely anyone there. It's only a matter of time before I need to face him again. But I don't need to look at him. *They don't pay me to look them in the eye.*

Still I can't help but notice his leather boots and padded jacket. Did he ride a motorcycle? It seems like that kind of leather, the tough kind. Meant to withstand weather. Meant to protect the body from impact.

The song's coming to a close, my routine is coming to an end and I'm glad about that. Something about this guy is throwing me off. Nothing noticeable. My feet and hands and knowing smile still land everywhere they need to. Muscle memory and all that. But I don't like the way he watches me.

There's patience in the way he watches me. And patience implies waiting.

It implies planning.

I reach back and unclasp my bra. I use one hand to cover my breasts while I toss the bra to the back of the stage. I pretend to be shy for a few seconds, and suddenly I feel shy too. Like I'm doing more than showing my breasts to strangers. I'm showing *him*. And as I stand there, hand cupping my breasts, breath coming fast, I feel his patience like a hot flame.

This time I do miss the beat. I let go on the next one, though, and my breasts are free, bared to the smoky air and the hungry eyes. There are a few whistles from around the room. Charlie holds up another five-dollar bill. I sway over to him and cock my hip, letting him shove the bill into my thong, feeling his hot, damp breath against my breast. He gets close but doesn't touch. That's Charlie. He tips and follows the rules, the best kind of customer.

I don't even glance at the other side of the room. If the new guy is holding up a tip, I don't even care. He doesn't seem like the kind of guy who follows rules. I don't know why I'm even thinking about him or letting him affect me. Maybe my run-in with Blue made me more skittish than I'd realized.

All I have left is my finale on the pole. I can get

through this.

This part isn't as physically strenuous as before. Or as long. All I really need to do is grind up against the pole, front and back, emphasizing my newly naked breasts, pretending to fuck.

That's what I'm doing when I feel it. Feel *him*.

I'm a practical girl. I have to be. But there's a feeling I get, a prickle on the back of my neck, a churning in my gut, a warning bell in my head when I'm near one of *them*. Near a cop. My eyes scan the back of the room, but all I can see are shadows. Is there a cop waiting to bust someone? A raid about to go down?

My gaze lands on the guy near the stage. Him? He doesn't look like a cop. He doesn't *feel* like a cop. But I don't trust looks or feelings. All I can trust is the alarm blaring in my head: *get out, get out, get out.*

I can barely suck in enough air. There's only smoke and rising panic. Blood races through me, speeding up my movements. *A cop.* I feel it like some kind of sixth sense.

Maybe he feels my intuition about him, because he leans forward in his seat.

In one heart-stopping moment, my eyes meet his. I can see his face then, drawn from charcoal shadows.

Beautiful, his lips say. All I can hear is the song.

I'm not even on beat anymore, and it doesn't matter. It doesn't matter because there's a cop here and I have to get out. Even if my intuition is wrong, it's better to get out. Safer.

I'll never be safe.

The last note calls for a curtsy—a sexy, mocking movement I choreographed into my routine. Like the one I'd do at the end of a ballet recital but made vulgar. I barely manage it this time, a rough jerk of my head and shoulders. Then I'm gone, off the stage, running down the hallway. I'm supposed to work the floor next, see who wants a lap dance or another drink, but I can't do that. I head for the dressing room and throw on a T-shirt and sweatpants. I'll tell them I feel sick and have to leave early. They won't be happy and I'll probably have to pay for it with my tips, but they won't want me throwing up on the customers either.

I run for the door and almost slam into Blue.

He's standing in the hallway again. Not slouching this time. There's a new alertness to his stare. And something else—amusement.

"Going somewhere?" he asks.

"I have to… My stomach hurts. I feel sick." I step close, praying he'll move aside.

He reaches up to trace my cheek. "Aww, should I call the doctor?" His hand clamps down on my shoulder. "I wouldn't want anything bad to happen to you."

I grip my bag tight to my chest, trying to ignore the threat in his words. And the threat in his grip. I really *do* feel sick now, but throwing up on him is definitely not going to help the situation. "Please, I need to leave. It's serious. I'll make it up later."

He'll know what I'm saying. That I'll make it up to

him personally. I'm just desperate enough to promise that. Desperate enough to promise him anything. And he's harassed me long enough that I know it's a decent prize. I'm sure he'll make it extra humiliating, but I'm desperate enough for that too.

"Please let me go." The words come out pained, my voice thin. It feels a little like my body is collapsing in on itself, steel beams bending together, something crushing me from the outside.

Regret flashes over his face, whether for refusing my offer or forcing me that low. But this time he doesn't let me go. "There's a customer asking for you. He wants a dance."

CHAPTER TWO

T HE GRAND USED to be a theater, back when the city did more tourist trade than drug trafficking. Back when you could walk down this street without getting mugged. They held ballets and operas and one infamous magic show where a man was killed by a faulty fake gun. Over the years the shows visited less and less. This whole part of the city became gutted, empty. Attempts to revitalize the theater failed because the good, rich folk who had money to spend on theater tickets didn't want to come to these streets.

Now the building is just a husk of its former glory— faded metallic wallpaper and ornate molding with the gold paint scraping off. Tables and chairs fill the smoky, dark floor. There is a balcony in the back, but it isn't open to the public.

The rooms for private dances used to be ticket stalls in what would have been the lobby.

They don't have doors. They barely even have walls. The front window partitions have been ripped away, with only brass rods and velvet curtains to cover them.

The first is occupied by Lola. A flash of red fabric and a long mane of hair between the curtain tells me that much. And I know from her position on the floor and the soft groans that he's paid for more than a dance.

The second room is empty.

The third room is the farthest from the main floor. The darkest. I can only make out a shadow seated in the chair. All I want is to get the hell out of here, but Blue is standing behind me, crowding me, and the only way to get space, the only place to go is inside.

I slip past the heavy velvet curtain and wait for my eyes to adjust. Even before they do, I know it will be him. Not safe, rule-following Charlie. It's the other man. The new one. The one with the strange intensity in his stare.

I see the outline of his jacket first. And his boots, forming that same configuration—one leg shoved out, one under the chair. That's the way he sits, almost sprawled on the uncomfortable wooden chair. He's watching me. Of course he's watching me. That's what he paid to do.

"What'll it be?" I ask.

"What's on the menu?" he counters, and I know what he means. He means extra services. The same thing that Lola is doing now. More than just a dance. He looks out from the shadows like the Cheshire cat, all eyes and teeth and challenge. All he's missing are purple stripes filling in.

And if he's a cop, he can bust me just for offering it. Cops should have better things to do with their time. But I already know cops don't do what they should. I know that too well.

I'm running from one.

"A dance, of course." I run through the prices for fifteen minutes, thirty minutes. No one needs longer than that. They either go to the bathroom to jerk off or come in their pants.

"And if I want more than that?"

Now that my eyes have adjusted, now that I'm up close, I can see the tats at the base of his neck and on his wrists. They are probably along his arms and maybe his chest. There's ink on his hands too, though I can't make out what it says.

His black shirt is tight enough to show me his shape, the broad chest and flat abs. Underneath the shirt is a chain or necklace. I can only see the imprint, but it makes me want to pull up the fabric and find out what it is.

He wears his leathers like a second skin, like they're armor and he's a fighter. I can't really imagine him walking through a precinct in a blue shirt. He's not a cop. But there was that feeling, when I was onstage. I *felt* his interest, more than sexual. I felt his suspicion. I felt every instinct telling me he is there for more than a dance. I can't afford not to listen.

"There's no more than that," I answer flatly.

He grunts, clearly displeased. But it doesn't sound like he's going to force the issue—or complain to Blue. "Then dance."

Right. That's why I'm here. That's not disappointment, heavy in my gut. I don't expect anything from men except to get paid. So I dance, starting slow, moving my hips, my arms, touching my breasts. I'm a million miles away like this. I'm lying on my back, feeling crisp grass underneath my legs, looking up at the night sky.

It almost works, except that I need to get close to him. I need to climb onto him, straddling his legs with mine, reaching for the back of the chair to shake my tits in his face. And when I do, I smell him. He smells…not like smoke. Not like sweat.

He smells like my daydream, like grass and earth and clean air.

I freeze above him, body crouched, my breasts still shivering with leftover momentum.

"Something wrong?" he asks.

And his voice. God, his voice. It's gone rough and low, all the way to the ground. It slides along the creaky wood of the chair and the concrete floor and vibrates up my legs. It shimmers through the air and brushes over my skin, that voice. We're not touching in any place, but I can feel him just the same.

I swallow hard. "Nothing's wrong, sugar."

"Then sit down."

He means on his lap. Touching. It's against the rules, officially.

Unofficially it's one of the tamer things that happen in this room. "What if I don't want to?"

One large shoulder lifts, making the leather sigh. "I won't make you."

I hear the unspoken word *yet* ring in the air.

I should probably refuse him. Whether he's a cop or not, he's throwing me off. That's dangerous. And if there's some other cop in the building? That's even more dangerous.

But for some reason, I lower myself until I'm resting on his jeans, my posture awkward and off balance—until he shifts, and suddenly I'm sliding toward him, flush against him while I straddle his legs. Then his arms circle my body, trapping me. Any second now he's going to grope me. Maybe take his dick out and fuck me like this. It wouldn't be the first time.

But he just stays like that, arms firm but gentle. A hug. This is a hug.

Jesus. How long has it been since a man hugged me? Just that, without touching anywhere else, without his dick inside me? A long time.

My throat feels tight. "What next?" I ask again, and this time I'll offer anything on the menu. The real menu, with sex and pain and whatever else he's into.

"I'd like to touch you," he says, his breath brushing against my temple.

I know that's not all. We haven't even negotiated a price, but I find myself agreeing, silent and still.

I look into his eyes and feel something—familiarity. Do I know him from somewhere?

A hundred men come through here. They are nothing to me, and yet I can't help thinking I would remember him if he had come in another night. I can't shake the feeling I've seen him before. Met him. *Known him.*

I should be afraid. And I am, but I'm also wondering about the tattoo on the back of his hand. What does it mean? Then I have other things to wonder about, because that hand is touching me.

He doesn't start with my breasts or even my ass. Not the obvious places, the important ones. He starts with one hand at the back of my neck. My heart pounds heavy in my chest, almost bursting free. I can't get enough air. And suddenly this seems like an important place after all, so vulnerable. So small within the careful hold of his hand. How is it possible that his hands are so large?

He slides his other hand under my chin, lifting my face. And looks me in the eye. I can't look away. His eyes are dark and bottomless, the light glinting like distant stars.

"What's your name?" he mutters.

Honor. I almost say it, but that's not who I am here. Besides, they announced me when I went onstage. He doesn't seem like the type to forget, not when he asked for me after, not with his hands cradling my head, careful with me but faintly threatening. Because he could snap my neck in a second. He knows it. I know it. I even think Blue waiting outside knows it, but it all comes down to trust.

And I don't trust him.

"Honey," I whisper.

He repeats my name like he's never heard of it before. "Honey."

My gaze drops to his mouth, which is firm and almost thin. A hard man's lips, with scruff shadowing his jaw. "And yours?"

Those lips curve into a half smile. "You're better off not knowing my name."

That much I believe. It makes me trust him more. "I'm better off not sitting on your lap. Better off not taking my clothes off for strange men every night. I guess that ship has sailed."

His lids lower with something like appreciation. "You can call me Kip." He must have seen I didn't quite believe him, because he laughs softly. "It's my real name. Not like Honey."

I wince at the pointed jab, but what does he expect? The truth?

There is no truth. Honey isn't my real name, but as each day goes by, I feel less and less like Honor Moretti. I'm transparent, like a ghost. Insubstantial. That's what hiding does to you. It makes you invisible.

He relents at whatever expression's on my face, softening. "It's short for Kipling."

Just those few words and he's given me something. Something personal. Something real. That's rare in this club. That's rare in the whole world. It makes me want more. I've seen the jut of old bone from the ground. I want to dig deeper, to uncover more truths. "As in Rudyard Kipling?"

His eyebrows rise. He tries to cover it up, but I've already seen.

"Are you surprised a stripper has read poetry?" I ask.

"No."

"Liar." I'm not mad though. The girls here are mostly surviving. We're kicking up to the surface. It doesn't leave a lot of leisure time for reading. "So, your parents were fans?"

"Just my mother, as far as I know." He gives a rueful smile like I've disarmed him. Which only proves he came here armed. "I'm just glad I got Kipling and not Rudyard."

I like him this way. More open. Less threatening. It eases me enough that I run my hands down his chest, drawing a shudder from him. "Did you grow up with Mowgli and Baloo?"

"Until I was sick of them," he says. "I had a big book, the kind you can only find in a garage sale. The paper yellow and the binding turning to string."

"It sounds lovely." My hands play lower—at the flat, hard plane at the bottom of his abs. Strippers often chat up the customers. Some of them come for more than a rub down. They want to talk, to flirt. They want to use us like therapists and then fuck us after. It's a kind of foreplay.

I tell myself that's why I'm talking to this man. No other reason. Not because I want to.

"It was," he says, "at the time. I'd get lost in them. I wanted to go live in the jungle."

"And then you grew up and realized you were already there."

His smile is pleased and sly. He likes this. "Is that where we are? The jungle?"

"The ground is made of concrete and the trees are full of glass. But there are snakes here. There are hunters."

"I thought it was just a story," he says lightly.

"Stories are powerful." They're life and death. They're survival. There wasn't much to do locked up in my room except read. And dance. I am a world away from that life, but that still holds true. I still spend most of my time reading and dancing.

And I'm still locked up, in a different way.

He looks too curious for my comfort. "So what stories do you tell?" he murmurs.

I shrug, for all the world nonchalant. "Same old story. Broken home. Ran away. Now I'm a stripper."

It's a sanitized version of the truth.

He frowns, uncertain, a furrow between his eyes. It makes him look younger than his scruff and his swagger and his size would indicate. Not like he feels sorry for me, though. Instead he looks like I'm a puzzle. Something to figure out.

The VIP room is really a miniature of the Grand. And his lap is my stage. His thighs are solid beneath my ass. I'm sitting, legs spread, arms at my side, chin up—totally open to him. It's dark here, but designed so he can look at my body up close. Except he's not looking at my body. He's looking at my eyes, and it almost takes my breath away, the wildness I glimpse in his.

And I need to take this spotlight off me. "So what do you want, Kip? What do you like?"

Dark lashes hide his eyes. "I'd like your real name."

"It's not for sale." And I'm still not sure why I wanted to tell him. It had almost slipped out. He's like a truth serum to me, and that's the most dangerous thing of all.

"Honey—"

"I'm here because you're paying me," I say, desperate to push him away. Desperate to hide. "Don't forget that."

He looks at me, and I watch his eyes harden. I can see the branches and brambles that he grows between us, feel the thorns where they push me out. He wants to dislike me. He wants to hate me. I don't know why, but I recognize the cold, hollow feeling in my gut when he looks at me. And I brace myself.

"You want to know what I like?" His gaze roams leisurely over my body. Then he looks me in the eye. "I want to fuck you, Honey. That's what I'd like."

My eyes fall shut. What is that feeling inside me? Relief? Disgust? It feels almost like gratitude. He wants to fuck, like every other guy wants. He's not here to expose my identity, not here to drag me back. He just wants to get his rocks off.

"That's not for sale either. I'm here to dance, to shake my tits. To rub them against you. That's it."

His eyes narrow. He doesn't like how crude I'm

being. He knows it's a weapon I'm wielding, but he's not injured. He's fighting back. Oh yes, there is something wild left in him. If he were in the jungle now, I'm not so sure he'd be the boy. He's much more likely a panther. Dangerous. A predator. "Hands or mouth, your choice."

"I said no."

"These rooms aren't just for dancing. I know that as well as you."

Yes, these rooms are for more than dancing, but that doesn't mean I do more. I don't have to, especially if I don't like the way the man treats me. That's a rule Ivan has for us. A twisted form of protection. I start to leave, but his hand squeezes the back of my neck. I grow still.

"I'm not going to hurt you," he says quietly.

Fear races through my veins. He's already hurting me, by holding me here when I want to leave. "Then what do you call this?" I whisper.

"Keeping you. For a little while. That's what you're here for, isn't it?"

God. He makes it sound so reasonable. But it's not. I know it's not. If it were any other man, I would have twisted away and run out of the booth. I would have been calling for Blue. We're a long way from the man who told me about poetry and childhood dreams, but I can't forget that he did. He's the same man, light and dark, petal and thorn. "Let me go," I say, my voice wavering, unsteady.

"Hands or mouth," he repeats.

I close my eyes. My eyes burn with unshed tears. I

don't want to cry. It's like waving a red flag at men like him. But the hands sliding down my body are surprisingly gentle. Over my abs and down to my…

"What are you doing?" I jerk away, but he's got one hand on my hip.

His eyes are dark, knowing. "If you won't decide, I will."

"I'm not going to blow you," I say, feeling small, like I've lost all control of the situation.

"I didn't tell you to," he says, one hand between my legs. The backs of his fingertips brush over my pussy. The thin strip of fabric over my pussy. "I want to fuck you with my fingers. I want to play with your clit until you come. Or maybe I'll slide my tongue over your pussy until you're crying loud enough for the whole club to hear, hmm? Your choice, Honey."

All the air rushes out of me. I don't know why it's so shocking. A blowjob is way dirtier than what he's asking for. But I've never had a man want to get me off. Typically they'd fumble around with my breasts, then come in my hands. I should tell him no again, like I did before. Blue would back me up. Ivan would protect me in this.

But there's a part of me intrigued by what he's offering. "Why?"

Amusement glints in his eyes. "The usual reasons."

It's so crazy I laugh, and my laugh sounds crazy too. "I'm not going to come, you know."

He considers this as he turns his hand and cups my

pussy. He isn't waiting until we've negotiated a price. He isn't waiting for permission. And I'm letting him. *Oh God.* He finds my clit with his thumb and gently circles.

He trails callused fingertips down my pussy and back up again. Slow. Focused. He seems to be making a study of me, mapping out my body. I've never had anyone go this slow, this careful. Never had hands so large be gentle.

"I wanted to touch you since I first saw you walk onto the stage. Whether I have to pay or not, whether you return the favor or not, I don't give a fuck. I'm going to finger this pretty cunt until you gush all over my hand. I'm going to keep going until you're slick with it, until my jeans are damp with you, until the scent of your sex is in the air."

I stare at him, somehow shocked, as if I've never heard these dirty words or witnessed these dirty acts. And I haven't—not the words in that order. Not with my body reacting, getting tight and wet for him. I think I actually might come for him.

"No," I whisper.

His fingers don't stop stroking me. If anything they slip in deeper. "That's what I want around my dick. Not your hands or your mouth. I want the juice from your pussy. When you're wet and coming, I'm going to dip my fingers inside your pretty pussy. I'll cover my dick with your juices, just like it would be if I fucked you bareback."

I could imagine him then, cock heavy with arousal,

glistening with my wetness. His cock would be large, like his hands and his whole body are large.

In the end it isn't his blunt fingers against my clit. Not even the dark, possessive gleam in his eyes. What pushes me over is the clean, earthy scent of him. I lean close, pressing my nose to his neck and breathing in deep as I come.

I stay there, pressed into every hollow place in him, somehow finding solace in the hard angles of his body. He is a mountain, and I am the shadows that fill every nook and cave around him.

Reality comes back to me, along with embarrassment. And confusion. I've never come in this room. Never in this building. God, I haven't even masturbated in forever—so worn down from hiding, so shamed by the place I'm hiding in, this strip club.

I'm hiding in him now.

How did he do this to me? One hour ago I had never seen this man, never imagined getting turned on in this dank room. Never sought comfort against rough, whisker-ticklish skin. He's changing me, teaching me to want more than survival.

Dangerous.

"Okay?" he asks, voice gruff.

Maybe he can tell I'm emotional. But if he thinks I need to feel dead inside to do my job, he's wrong. Lola is the strong one, the one who performs without feeling a thing. Candy does it too, even if she needs drugs to manage it. But I've never been able to find that numbness. I feel it all—every insult, every grope. Every cock. And now I would feel his thick cock too.

That doesn't seem like the worst thing.

"How do you want me?" My voice trembles, but that doesn't stop him.

His fingers are cupping my pussy, unmoving, letting me recover. Now he dips his finger inside, where I am the most sensitive and wet. Then he lifts his hand to my mouth. One stroke, painting my lips with my arousal, heating up every nerve ending. His head dips, and I know what's coming next. But I don't turn my face away. I don't tell him kisses aren't for sale.

I let him taste me on my lips. He licks the wetness, a slow swipe of his tongue that makes me gasp. My lips part, and he takes full advantage. His tongue pushes inside, opening me. His hand at the back of my neck is my only anchor while his mouth claims mine.

It's almost too much. Too intense.

"*How do you want me?*" I'm demanding this time. I need to know. Because I need to stop this strange intimacy that only increases with every murmured word and tender touch.

"What are you afraid of, sweetheart?"

My eyes widen. How does he know?

Maybe he's not really that perceptive. Maybe all the men that come through here can see I'm terrified, but they don't care as long as I make them hard.

"How do you want me?" My voice is hoarse, pleading. *This is all I have to give. Take it.*

His jaw tightens. "I want you like this. Spread open. Waiting for me to do whatever I want to you."

His hand returns to my pussy, and I feel relief. Disappointment too. It hurts that he's stopped kissing me, because for some reason I liked it. And I know, most likely, it won't happen again. Not tonight. Not ever again. But it's for the best. I shouldn't get used to this.

He pulls more wetness from my core and paints my nipples—first one, then the other. I shiver under his touch. It's more like shaking, really. Because I know what comes next, the same thing he did to my mouth.

He pulls me up so my breasts are in front of his face. He licks the wetness off my nipple, sucks me until I moan. Then he gives my other breast the same treatment.

And I can't say anything. Can't demand to know how he wants me. He dips his fingers one more time, deep inside me, pulling out all the wetness he can find. I clench around his fingers and hear his breath catch.

He doesn't put my arousal on my body, not this time. Slowly, deliberately, he unbuckles his pants and pulls himself out. He's as hard as I imagined. As big. As slick at the tip. He runs a fist down his length, mixing my arousal with his precum over his cock.

I can't say anything, but I don't have to. *How do you want me?* I know how he wants me, and I slide to the floor. The floor that's cold and dusty and damp at the same time, unforgiving against my shins. I'm more comfortable here. Safer. Because this *is* for sale. And I have the upper hand now. Sex is a battlefield, and this concrete floor is my country to defend.

"What's your name?" His voice is low—and desperate? That can't be right. He doesn't need anything from me. He could have gone to a bar. With that hard jaw and hard body, he would have had his pick. Any girl would have hopped on the back of the motorcycle I suspect he has. And yet he's here.

He can pay for my mouth. He can even pay for my orgasms. He doesn't get my name.

"Honey."

He laughs, a little coarse, a little bitter. But his eyes, they understand. They're almost soft, tender as they look down at me kneeling. "Pretty little liar."

But when I lean forward to take him in my mouth, he pushes me away. He fists his cock, fucking himself, still slick from my pussy. He's taking himself fast and hard—almost like a punishment.

He took his time with me, but not with himself. Now he races himself to the finish line, fist and hips at war until he tenses and comes, spilling into his own hand while I kneel before him and watch.

He collapses back onto the chair, still sprawled but truly relaxed now. Not tense or wary. Not carefully banked power like I felt before. Now he is an animal in repose, a lion spread across a rock, bathing in the sun— even if the rock is a creaking wooden chair, straining under his force. Even if the sun is the flicker of fluorescent lights from the edges of the velvet curtain. It's still primal.

Still beautiful.

His eyes are closed. His head falls back.

And for some reason I almost tell him my name. I form it with my lips and tongue, but he can't see. I don't know why I'd ever tell him…except that I want someone to see me here. To know me here. So that I don't have to feel alone.

But he isn't here to know me. He isn't here to save me either.

Alertness breathes into him again. His expression is sated and…grateful. "C'mere," he says on a grunt.

And before I can do what he says, he lifts me into his lap. He tucks my legs over the side of his and kisses me—slow, languid swipes of his tongue against mine.

I push away from him, staggering back. I don't have my balance yet, but it doesn't matter. I shove aside the velvet curtain and run. He hasn't paid me, but I don't care.

"What the hell?" Blue asks, grabbing my arm.

But I break free and keep running. I don't care what happens behind me. I don't care about Kip or the fact that I'll never see him again.

It's better if I don't.

I read my mother's diary until the day she left. That's how I knew about her affair with the guards. More than one, although it was the last man who got her killed. She thought she loved him.

And she was planning to leave my father.

In that diary I saw her ticket to Tanglewood, West Virginia. There were two words scrawled on the ticket—*The Grand*. I'd never heard of it then, but it became a kind of North Star for me. As a teenager I had to stay with my family.

And when I'd finally run, I'd known just where we'd go.

I just hadn't known it was a strip club until I arrived.

CHAPTER THREE

A STRANGER LOOKS at me from the mirror.

Black thong and red lipstick. They're my costume, but sometimes it feels like I don't need them. I've been hiding long enough that it feels more natural than honesty. My green eyes and black hair and pale skin are a costume too. I use them to disguise myself when I strip—just another set of tits and ass. How deep does that costume go?

Is there anything underneath?

I'm not sure anymore.

Lola crosses the room toward me. I watch her in the mirror, even when she perches on my vanity table. She wears some kind of red-leather strap bodice that shows more skin than it covers. It looks sexy and almost alien. "What happened?" she asks.

I blink. "What do you mean?"

"Don't play dumb. That's Candy's routine. I know something's eating you. And I know you left early last night. Some guy get fresh?"

Yeah, some guy had gotten fresh. But it had happened before and never affected me like this. It's a good sign that she doesn't know what happened though. It means Blue probably collected the money and made excuses for me. I'll owe him one now. "I wasn't feeling well."

Her expression is knowing—and sympathetic. It's the sympathy that hurts the most. "If you want to talk about it…"

I don't want to talk about Kip and how strange he made me feel. Lola doesn't even know why I'm here, who I'm running from—and I want to keep it that way. She doesn't know any of my secrets.

"Where's Candy?" I say instead.

"*If you want to talk about it,*" she says more sternly, "I'm here. The offer stands. And anyway, maybe there's something going around, because Candy didn't show today either."

But Lola and I both know there isn't any real sickness. "Did she call in?"

"No, but you know Candy."

I do know Candy. I know she sometimes goes home with guys who promise her a good time, even though Ivan has rules about that. I know for Candy *a good time* means alcohol or drugs or both. It's a dangerous game she plays, but I can't judge. I just worry. "Maybe we can stop by after our shift."

Lola snorts. "And get attacked in that fucking rat trap she lives in? No, thanks. I'd rather get attacked here. At least then I get paid."

All the girls live in crappy places, but Candy's place is actually the worst. Part of the ceiling in the hallway has just caved in, and there are always guys sitting in the stairwells. It looks more like an abandoned building that squatters use.

I kind of can't believe she pays to live there. "Maybe if she doesn't show up tomorrow, we'll go."

"She'd better show up tomorrow. Ivan's already pissed."

Shit shit shit.

Dread forms a large knot in my stomach. Ivan is our boss, and the second-scariest man I've ever met. Maybe Blue did tell on me. Though Ivan doesn't visit often, and it seemed weird that he'd come just because I'd left early. And also acted strange with a customer, running out before getting paid. But even if I wasn't the reason for his visit, I still might get in trouble now that he's here.

Another part of me tensed in anticipation. Maybe he had information for me.

"Ivan's here?"

"Just talked to him in his office." Lola winks. "Oh, did I not mention? He wants to see you."

✧　✧　✧

If the Grand is the murky underwater, then the basement office is the sea bottom, far enough down that no light can reach. The railing keeps me from tripping and falling down the stairs. At the small landing, I knock on the door and wait.

There's a framed painting of the Grand hanging on the wall. Its brick was once a deep, startling red. For some reason, the painting hasn't faded, entombed here in the basement. But the real brick did fade. It turned dark the way blood does when it dries. That's all the building is to the city now—a scab.

A minute passes, and then I hear Ivan inside. "Enter."

When I go inside, it's the opposite of a stage. There are no spotlights to blind me. Just a dim stillness to wade through. The room is mostly unfinished, with a concrete floor and exposed vents from the ceiling. It's the kind of place where I wouldn't be surprised to find a person hanging in chains in the corner. A dungeon.

There have never been chains down here. I have an overactive imagination.

Or maybe a good memory, of a different time and place.

"Mr. Kosta," I say.

"Sit." He doesn't look up from the paper he's reading.

I'm not sure how the small lamp provides enough light to see by, but he's absorbed in his work. Then his gaze flicks to me, and I understand. Because his pale blue eyes are like spotlights, making me feel exposed.

"How are you, Honey?"

I suppress a shiver.

The first time we met, I came to him for a favor. I needed information. Why had my mother planned to come here? What was waiting for her here? And some small part of me still hoped she'd arrived, that she'd escaped some other way.

Ivan had made me dance for him.

He watched me impassively. The hardness in his suit pants told me he liked what he saw, but his eyes were flat. He made no comment on my body, made no move to touch me. Instead he said I would work at his club. I would only have to dance. Not fuck anyone. And in return he would look for the information I needed. He was the most well-connected man in this old city.

And he named me Honey. Similar to my own name, but the opposite really.

I hate the name, and I think he knows that. It's a hammer. Every time I hear it, I sink a little deeper into the wood.

I think he knows that too.

"Fine, sir," I say now.

That earns me a faint smile. "So respectful. Are you this respectful with everyone?"

Yes. I've always been the good girl. "I don't know."

I remember avoiding Blue's gaze. I remember kneeling at Kip's feet. I probably do look respectful, but mostly I feel afraid. Maybe those are the same things.

"Do you know why I called you down?"

I shake my head, hopeful. "You found something?"

"Yes." He leans back and crosses one ankle over his knee. "But that's not the only reason. Someone was asking about you."

My throat seems to close up entirely. I can almost hear the metal clang of a gate falling around me, trapping me where I sit. He already knows way more about me than is safe. I had to tell him in order to stay here. Had to tell him to get the information I need. Had to tell him to keep my sister safe. *Clara.*

If he tells someone else, I'm fucked. And so is she.

"Who? When? What did you tell them?" My words come out soft, almost like a shuddery breath. That's all I can do now. Count my breaths and stare down the barrel.

"I told them you're one of my girls." One corner of his mouth lifts. "I told them you're valuable to me. And loyal. Aren't you?"

All I can think about is running again. That's the opposite of loyalty. "Yes."

He laughs softly. "You're a nice girl. A good girl. You've always done what I need you to. I like to reward good behavior."

Does he mean information? Protection? The former is why I'm here. But the latter... God, we need protection. I can't imagine he would do that. No matter how much I earn onstage, it isn't worth using his resources to guard me. No, I can't rely on Ivan.

We've been found. We're in danger. My mind is already mapping bus routes out of the city. Where would I go next? Far. That's the answer.

As far as the money I'd earned stripping would last.

He looks thoughtful. "You'll be safe enough here. His name is Kip. And I think..." A smile now. "I think he wants to fuck you."

Relief pours through me, so hot and potent I feel faint with it. I can't even be angry that Ivan has been taunting me with this. It's not Byron. It's not my father. It's just a man interested in a stripper—*nothing special here, move along.* "I've danced for him."

Ivan's eyes narrow. "Interesting. Actually, I found something you might be interested in. In my own records. It turns out the man you asked about used to work here. Security. This was before I came to own the place. From the file I have, he'd been fucking around with the girls one time too many."

I flinch. That is the man my mother had believed herself in love with. That is who she'd gotten killed for. "When did he stop working here?"

Ivan reads off a date from a paper on his desk.

I imagine this man getting fired and looking for work elsewhere. He could have gotten a job with my father in a different state. He had fallen in love with my mother— or at least pretended to. They'd hatched the plan to steal the jewels. He never could have pulled it off alone. My mother would have helped him.

An inside job all the way.

A few days later my father told me she was in a car accident, even though she wasn't allowed to leave the mansion any more than I was. She certainly wasn't allowed to drive herself. It was clearly a lie, but what was he hiding? Her murder? Or her escape?

A man with his pride might have said that to save face. I'm here because of simple, stupid hope. Maybe she did use that ticket to leave Las Vegas. Maybe she's still alive. Maybe she's living in a cute little house with her lover—with spare bedrooms for me and Clara.

Okay, that last part is just a fantasy. But there's something here in this city. The jewels? The truth? I need to find out if my mother made it here. I need to find out what happened to her.

"My mother?" I ask.

He shakes his head. *No. Not yet.*

And I need to keep stripping if I want him to keep looking.

"Can I go now?" I whisper. It's a weakness, I know that. If I were stronger, I could bluff. I'd pretend I didn't care and walk out with a flick of my hair, like Candy can do.

I'm not bluffing though. I can't. My whole body is a tell—tense and terrified.

"Why would I keep you?" The question isn't innocent. He doesn't mean *I'd never keep a woman against her will.* He means, *You're valuable to me. I can use you.* His casual tone is a block of cheese set inside a trap, something to lure me inside. I'm a mouse in a lion's den. He's playing with me. It's only a matter of time until he pounces. But if I leave the cave, I give up any chance of keeping Clara safe.

We'd be found eventually, but we wouldn't have the leverage to fight my father.

My chest is tight. "I'm doing what you asked me to. Dancing." *Fucking.*

In that, he's just like Byron. Just like my father. They want my body. They want vacant eyes and a small clay smile. They want a doll.

He nods, accepting my obedience as if it's his due. "And I'll keep looking for information on your mother. But I want you to stay away from Kip."

What? I stare back, silent. It's bad enough to have to dance for these men at the flick of his fingers. Now I have to stop. There's something deeper going on here. Why does he know Kip but dislike him? He seems almost afraid... and yet, he's the most dangerous man here.

So what does that make Kip?

Ivan smiles, predatory. "It's interesting that he's here at all, but then you're an interesting woman. I knew that the first time I saw you, when you showed up desperate for a job and much too thin. But you certainly know how to make the customers hard, don't you, Honor?"

I flinch, more because he uses my real name than anything else.

I can't deny that I was desperate. I'd have done anything for this job, but Ivan's never fucked me, never touched me. He's never watched me dance beyond the initial interview I did for him. In that respect I've been lucky to be here. But I know male appreciation when I see it. If I have to use that to stay off the grid, I will. If I have to use it to save Clara, I will.

After all, that's what I've been doing all this time.

"I'll do anything." I'm not even sure what I'm begging for. Answers? Sanctuary?

But he seems to know. His eyebrows rise. "How about giving me your sister?" A beat. "No? I didn't think so."

I swallow hard. He doesn't want my sister, not really. He wants me desperate.

And that's what he'll get.

I can do this. Hadn't I just done the same thing last night? But it feels different, when I stand up. It feels different because when I did this to Kip, I wanted to. No matter what I told myself, it hadn't been fear I'd felt behind that velvet curtain. Not fear of him, anyway. I'd felt desire, and that was the scariest thing of all.

I don't feel desire now, but I still know how to move my hips, how to kneel in front of him, how to run a hand across his thigh. His legs part to give me access, but I need more permission before I can continue. Overstepping my bounds with a man like him can be fatal.

"Let me," I whisper.

Let me touch him, suck him. *Let me go.*

He catches my chin between his thumb and forefinger, forcing me to look him in the eye—in a similar position to what Kip had been in last night. But Kip's dark eyes had been hungry and warm and concerned.

Ivan just looks curious, as if I were an animal performing some mating act he finds faintly distasteful. "If you suck me off, what then? You'll walk out that door, and I'll lose one of my best dancers."

I flinch, unable to deny the truth.

If he let me go now, I'd be gone. On the run, again and always. But if Ivan has figured that out, then he won't let me go. My stomach turns over.

He smiles. "I want something far more valuable than a blowjob, Honor. I want you. Here. And under my control. So don't bother running. I'd only find you. Unless the person you're running from finds you first."

I stand to leave. I'd have run if I needed to. I'd have fought if he made me. But he leans back in his chair, apparently content to let me go for now. I hurry to the door.

"Oh, and Honey?"

I pause, feeling small. He knows. *He likes it that way.*

"Kip and I go way back. Let's just say, he's not someone you want to fuck with."

Oh, and you are? I just nod briefly—a jerk of my head. Acknowledging the truth of it.

"Stay away from him," he says. It's not a suggestion. It's an order.

CHAPTER FOUR

I IMAGINE MYSELF on a bus heading somewhere far away. Except if I leave, I know Ivan will find me. And in the process, he'll kick over every rock until *everyone* knows where to find me. I'm trapped just as surely as when I left. Unless I stay here and keep my head down, earn more money, stay safe another few days...and maybe find out what happened to my mother. Doesn't she deserve justice? Doesn't she deserve peace?

Clara deserves it, that's for sure. Finding those jewels means peace. It's a long shot, but so is staying alive. Survival is a long shot when you have dangerous men hunting you. And dangerous men ordering you around.

Ivan ordered me to stay away from Kip, but somehow I'm standing here in front of the velvet curtain. I'm wearing full gear tonight for the floor. That means a lacy black bra and panties, just begging to be ripped off in front of some panting guy, in the dark recesses of a VIP room. I feel shaky, like I might throw up. It's not stage fright. It's the opposite. I can dance in front of a roomful of men. But the thought of being enclosed with this one is making my heart pound.

I glance back, but Blue is busy with some guy who

got too up close and personal with Lola. I could wait for him to be finished and then tell him Ivan won't let me see this guy. Blue isn't about to disobey an order like that. But on some level I don't want Blue to step in. I don't want to listen to Ivan.

I want to go inside.

My palms grow hot. I know he'll be sprawled on the chair, one long leg kicked out, the other tucked back. I know he'll be wearing the scuffed boots and leather jacket. I know exactly how he'll smell—like musk and danger, like salt and spice.

When I slip past the curtain, a slow grin spreads across his face. It looks like a smile I'd see when I open the door for a date, both appreciative and a little surprised. It should be out of place in the dark, dank VIP room, but my heart flutters anyway.

Damn it. I'm determined to make this time different.

"Hey, sugar," I say in a voice so smooth and practiced it is clearly false. "I'm glad to see you."

He doesn't need to know that I actually am glad to see him again. Or that I find him sexy.

His smile fades a little. Apparently the seductress play isn't what he's expecting. Last time I'd been bumbling and awkward and, worst of all, real. I won't make that mistake twice.

He studies me like I'm a puzzle. *I'm the simplest thing you'll ever see,* I want to tell him. *I'm afraid.* But I smile instead. It's not a big smile, not real, but it's pretty. I know exactly what it looks like in the mirror, with my makeup on. I give it to him the same way I give him my time and my body—by the hour.

"What'll it be tonight, sugar?" I ask.

A little crease forms between his eyebrows. My fingers twitch. I want to smooth it away. And then I'd keep going, running my fingertip over those thick eyebrows, trailing my hand down his bristly cheek. I shave and pluck the hairs on my body, leaving my skin smooth. But he has all his hair—he's covered in the stuff. It looks both soft and coarse, both attractive and forbidding.

"Can I talk to you?" he asks quietly.

This was what I'd been afraid of. Niceness. Curiosity. It's not good, coming from a customer. It's not good coming from anyone. "We're talking right now, sugar."

"Come here." He pulls his leg even, making it clear he wants me on his lap. I remember that lap, his thighs strong and warm and thick under me. I had an orgasm on that lap.

I can't risk it. So I slide to the floor instead, glancing up at him with a seductive smile. My breasts sway as I crawl toward him in the small space. I move like a cat, rubbing against him before flicking my ass. His gaze roams my body, hovering on each part, unable to choose a place to land. He likes my breasts and my belly, my ass and my legs.

Then he looks back at my face, locking his eyes on mine. "I said come here."

He doesn't let me get away with much. I can feel the invisible leash around my neck. I can feel him tug. I slip between his legs. It's close enough to his lap that I can pretend innocence. Maybe this was what he meant all along. I give lap dances all night long, but very few men will turn down a blowjob if I'm already kneeling between their legs.

I slide my hands up his thighs, staring at the bulge in his jeans. He wants this, and somehow so do I. I don't have any illusions about blowjobs. I don't imagine it will taste good or feel sexy, but I want to hear him fall apart. I want to feel it.

His hands grab my wrists. His eyes are dark now, displeased.

He pulls. My body swings up, easy and lightweight in his arms. Then I'm in his lap, tucked into the crook of his arm, straddling his legs. *Shit.*

I force myself to pout, to keep things lighthearted. "I want to make you feel good, sugar."

His arms tighten around me, half embrace and half prison. "You do."

My heart pounds. He pushes past my defenses, just like that. Not with cruelty. That I could manage. Or at least, survive. He slips underneath my walls just by looking at them. I don't know what would happen if he actually did more. How quickly I would fall.

And I want him to feel just as vulnerable—more. So I relax my body, as if I'm giving in. I rest my arms on his shoulders, either side. My palms slide down his chest to frame the necklace he wears, the one underneath his shirt.

"What's this?" I whisper.

His expression closes. "It's nothing."

I recognize those walls—I put them up myself. And I recognize those lies. They are all I have left. That alone should make me respect his wishes. I can suck his dick without lifting his shirt. Instead I find myself stroking his neck, reaching down to the warm metal chain—and pulling out the necklace.

A cross. A simple cross with straight lines, formed out of a black stone with cloudy white swirling through. Marble? I think he must have worn it for a long time. But somehow I know I am one of the only people to ever see it.

Because he let me see it. I don't fool myself. He could have stopped me. He could do *anything* to me, but he let me take out his necklace. The unexpected trust sits on my chest, making it hard to breathe.

"I didn't take you for a religious man." It isn't only his presence here in the strip club. Hypocrisy runs deep. I wouldn't be surprised to find half the men here in church on Sundays, wiping away their sins with the same hands and tongues they used to defile me.

But he has something they don't, a kind of fight, a stark determination that says he walks his own path. He has his own plan—and no use for God's.

"I'm not religious," he says, tucking the cross back under his shirt. "That's a gift."

It has to be from a woman. While the shape of it is simple, almost primitive, it was clearly chosen with love and feminine affection. And it certainly matches Kip's dark looks—his black boots and black jacket. His black eyes. They're angry now, but I don't stop. A wise woman would leave him alone. She would take her clothes off. She'd give him her body. But she'd never trust him with her heart.

"Who gave this to you?" I whisper. His mother? A girlfriend?

His wife?

I tell myself it doesn't matter. Plenty of men here are married. Rings are common enough, worn by men too lazy or brazen to take them off before coming. But I don't want this man to be married.

His expression darkens. "You want answers, but you won't give me any. Fair's fair, sweetheart."

I flinch as his hand reaches for me, but he only tucks a lock of hair behind my ear. It's always coming undone from the pins I use to hold it. My hair is always falling down around me, tumbling and wild. The admiration in his eyes says he likes it that way. His hand lingers in my hair, teasing the strands between his fingers.

"Tell me your name," he says gently. "If you don't trust me, I can't help you."

Every muscle freezes. Cold sweeps in, turning me to ice. I don't feel fear. I can't feel pain. "How do you know I need help?"

His eyes soften. The understanding in them is like a physical blow, and I have to hold my breath just to keep myself from shattering.

"Don't you?" He strokes rough fingers down my cheek. "Your eyes ask for help. Your body. You look down at me from the stage like you want me to climb up and take you away."

I stare at him, shocked. Shocked that he read so much into me. Shocked that he's right. "*No.*"

His large hand wraps the back of my neck. He tugs me close and whispers in my ear, "What are you afraid of?"

My heart pounds so loud it's all I can hear. The dark walls become blurry as if I'm going fast instead of trapped. As if I'm falling. "I don't need your help. This is where I want to be."

He looks around like he's just noticed our surroundings. Sharp eyes don't miss anything—not the grit on the floor or the desolation in my lie. "This is where you want to be," he says. "This hellhole. Is that right?"

I laugh suddenly. It takes me by surprise. "This isn't hell. You think heaven is nice clothes and expensive locks? That's what hell is made of."

Then there's knowledge in his eyes. "And you left that…for this."

"I don't need your pity." It makes me angry, the way he's looking at me. I don't want him to feel sorry for me. I want him to desire me again. I want to see him panting after me again. "What I need is for you to stop talking and start fucking. You can do that, right? That's what you're here for, isn't it?"

His hand tightens in my hair. For a moment I think

he's going to call my bluff. In that moment, I want him to. Instead he tugs downward, guiding me to the floor.

Now he'll fuck my mouth, won't he? He'll use me, just like I wanted.

But he doesn't do that.

Instead he pushes his boot between my legs. His hand remains in my hair, holding me there. I'm straddling his leg, bracing myself with my hands on his thighs. Is he going to... kick me? But there isn't really room for that. There isn't room for much of anything, except the solid warmth of his leg holding me up. I've had my legs spread, my ass up, my mouth around a stranger's cock—but I've never felt quite as vulnerable as I do now.

"What are you going to do to me?" My voice trembles. I can't even find it in me to care. Pride is a thing of the past. Pride is silk and good wine—things I can no longer afford.

"What you asked for." He looks angry now, but his touch is still gentle as he shifts me lower. I'm hugging his leg now, the warm leather of his boot pressed right against my pussy. "You wanted us to fuck. You wanted me to pay you for it. Well, this is how I want you."

A pain in my scalp drags me up, and then I'm rocking back down again. Up and then down—he gives me the rhythm to move. It's sex, that rhythm.

It's dancing.

I'm already in a strip club. There should be nothing dirtier I can do, nothing lower. But now I'm grinding on this man's boot, feeling horrible pleasure spark in my clit, and I realize I was wrong. This is worse. This is dirtier by far.

"Wait," I whimper even though I don't know what we'd wait for.

His hand drops, heavy on my shoulder, squeezing gently. "No, baby. This is what you asked for, and I'm giving it to you. That's how this works."

"This isn't..." My throat feels tight, and horrible tears prick my eyes. I didn't cry when I danced onstage the first time. Didn't cry when I got fucked. Why does he make me feel like this? It's even worse than how Byron made me feel. "This isn't using me. It's not making you feel good."

A rough laugh, like metal dragging over concrete. "Oh, I'm feeling pretty good, sweetheart."

He means his erection. He means the sizable bulge in his jeans.

"Let me stroke you," I beg him. Anything would be easier than getting raked over his boot, fucking his leg, exposed in my own awkward arousal. It's building even though I know this is wrong. No, it's building faster *because* it's so wrong. There's something perverse in me. I don't know if I was born with it or if Byron drilled it into me, but the humiliation only makes me hotter. Every stroke of the supple leather to my clit brings a new rush of heat.

He shakes his head, the expression in his eyes almost sad. "This is what you asked for," he repeats. "Maybe next time you'll ask for what you need."

I shudder, right on the edge. "I need, I need—"

"I know," he murmurs.

As I look into his eyes, I have the strangest feeling that he *does* know. Maybe he already knows what I'm afraid of. Maybe he knows what I need. It pushes me over, and then I'm coming, rocking my clit against leather, humping his leg while he murmurs how good I am, how sweet.

And when I am done, my body trembling, heart thudding, he pays me. I stare at the money as if I've never seen it before—as if I've never gotten paid before. As if it's never hurt this bad before.

His expression is hungry as he stares down at me. But I must not be enough, because his erection is still thick in his jeans when he stands.

He looks down at me, and I feel again those brambles grow wild and fast, foliage too dense to see past, branches too thick to cut down. And again, that strange sense that he wants to hate me. He doesn't want to get close. I remember this feeling too well. And when Kip leaves, I shiver on the floor, nauseous and afraid, remembering.

✧   ✧   ✧

Six months ago

MY FACE IS stiff from smiling. My calves ache from the

four-inch heels. Why is it the more a shoe costs, the thinner its sole? I greet another couple with as much warmth as I can pretend, considering the man has a lipstick smear on his face.

Not the same shade as his wife's lipstick.

These parties are see and be seen. Fuck and be fucked. The woman scans the room as we discuss the latest charity fundraiser. She's looking for her next conquest.

"Honor, darling." The voice is like a cube of ice all the way down my spine.

I turn to greet the handsome man. Byron Adams, my fiancé. And the rising star in the Las Vegas Police Department. He's aiming for police commissioner. "Byron, I was wondering where you'd gotten to."

There is no lipstick on his face, which isn't proof of anything. No, the main reason I believe he is faithful is because of the look in his eye. The one that scares me. "I was talking business," he says with an almost bashful smile. It was strange to see that expression on him. It made him seem younger. It made me ache. "And missing you."

Both the man and woman smile at us like we're in love. I have to remember that. We *are* in love.

I lay my hand on his arm and force a smile. "Then take me with you."

And he does. He leads me out of the room and up the stairs to the office. I've been in this office a thousand times, but not like this. Not with my fiancé's rough hands bending me over the desk. He drags up the hem of my glittery dress, exposing my ass. The thong snaps.

"I couldn't find you," he says, voice tight.

There's no right answer. If he wants me, he gets me. "I'm sorry," I murmur, pleading.

The sound of a zipper pierces the room. Then he is inside me, skin to skin. His cock thrusts deep into my cunt. The papers are probably important, the tally of millions of dollars, but I crush them in my fists.

His fingers dig into my hips. "I don't like that. Stay where I can see you."

"I will," I gasp out, but it's hard. Hard because I can barely breathe, the way he's thrusting faster now. Harder. The way my face is shoved into the desk, leaving streaks of eye makeup on the crinkled sheets of paper, damp with tears.

We are in love.

He pulls out. I tense up, knowing what's coming next. If I'd had any doubts—any hopes—they are gone when he spits onto my ass. Careless fingers smooth the saliva into my puckered hole. Then his cock is pressing against me.

I practice like he tells me to. The plugs are as big as I can bear, but it's still too much. Too much when his cock is inside me, dragging against the tender flesh, fucking me.

"Wait," I whimper. "Wait."

I don't mean *wait.* I mean *no no no.* I mean *stop and never start again.* It doesn't matter. He doesn't stop, and that's for the best. If he did, he'd ask what I meant. He'd ask why I said it. And I don't have answers for him. I only have my own muffled groans as he slams back into me.

I only have pain as he presses deep.

CHAPTER FIVE

THE REST OF the night I dance in a kind of trance, only vaguely aware of the flashing lights or the applause. The hands that reach for me, stroking and grabbing, barely register tonight. The hurt and shame I feel after being made to fuck his boot are too strong. I can see why Candy likes to shoot up before she goes onstage. I wish she was here so I could ask her for a hit.

There's shock too, and that helps.

It's dreamlike. I'm not really here, undressing and shaking my ass for strangers. I'm not even awake.

The sky is already a murky orange by the time I leave. A fine mist hangs between the buildings, a cross between fog and morning dew. The Grand is closing. Blue is ejecting the last customers, and they wander away, tripping their way over the uneven cobblestones, bleary and already hungover. Half the stones in the driveway are gone, pieces of the building's façade missing, as if we're in some battle-torn country. And we are. Wars are fought and lost on this street.

The well of the central fountain contains only dried leaves and cigarette butts. Whatever statuette once adorned the center pillar has long since been cracked off, leaving only a jagged edge jutting up. It's a fitting centerpiece for the courtyard and the Grand as a whole, broken and proud.

I'm still in a trance as I head to Candy's apartment. The numbness helps me here too, dulling my fear as I step over the bums and scary-looking men slumped over in the stairwell.

My knock echoes off the faded green walls.

She doesn't answer.

"Candy," I say, pressing my face against the door, hoping she'll hear me. Still no answer. I try the doorknob just in case, but it's locked.

Worry churns in my stomach. If she OD'ed on something behind that door…if she went home with some guy and he tied her up in the basement… there are so many ways she could get into trouble. So many ways to get hurt.

I know that from experience.

"Candy." This time it's a whisper. I know she won't answer. Whether she's high or just gone, she's beyond my reach.

Silly to think I could help her, when I can't even help myself.

I climb over the men on the stairs, hopeless and distracted. I almost don't notice the man who holds the door open for me. In fact I'm already turning toward the sidewalk outside Candy's apartment when I feel the prickle on the back of my neck. The same one I felt the first night he showed up at the strip club.

I freeze. Every muscle in my body locks tight.

"I'm not going to hurt you," comes a masculine murmur behind me. A *familiar* male voice.

My heart pounds. My hands clench around the handle of the duffel bag.

"Honey," he says softly. And there's none of the mocking this time, even though the name is fake. He sounds mostly concerned.

Oh God, it's him. I'd hoped I was wrong. He may say he's not going to hurt me, but no man shows up uninvited to a stripper's room with good intentions. I don't turn, don't face him. I speak to the empty sidewalk instead. "What are you doing here?"

"I followed you." He pauses. "It's not safe here."

A chill runs over my skin. How did I miss him? And what else have I missed? Time on the run has given me certain skills, but I'm not a spy. I'm an heiress. A *principessa.* At least that's what I was trained to be. I can host a dinner party for the most wealthy, lethal men in the country, but I don't know how to spot a tail. I don't know how to fight one.

I swallow hard. "What do you want from me?"

A blowjob? A fuck? These are the only things I have to give.

His sigh caresses my temple, gently ruffling my hair. "I just want to talk."

That makes me scoff. He may stalk me, and I may fuck him, but at least we can be honest about it. "Then why are you in my space?"

Politeness is a ten-dollar bill tossed onto the stage. But for this, stalking and holding open the door in a parody of gentlemanly manners, he can get out of my personal space. He can stop making my heart beat too fast and my skin feel clammy and hot.

After a pause, he steps back. Not far, but enough that I can breathe again. I turn to face him—and again I'm struck with that sense of déjà vu, of recognition. Have I met him before? I would remember that face, the hardness of his features, the hint of vulnerability in his dark eyes, but all I have is a strange feeling, like I trust him even though he's a stranger.

Obviously it's a feeling I can't trust.

I consider running for it, as useless as that would be. He's too fast for me. And I don't want to see what he's like when he gets rough. And besides, I'd run the risk of leading him to the motel room—and to Clara.

It's not like I could call the cops on him—at least not without answering a lot of other uncomfortable questions. Instead I let him ease the duffel bag away from me when he moves to take it from me. Without asking, of course. He slings it over his shoulder in a dark parallel to chivalry. He'll let me go when he's ready to.

"I'm not going to hurt you." His gaze remains on me as we stand in front of Candy's shit-hole apartment building. This building, this ground had seen violence before. I can feel it vibrate through the concrete. And it probably will again—I just hope it won't be today.

I press my hands together, hating how helpless I feel.

"Then let's walk. In public."

When he doesn't answer, I head back toward the club. He falls in step beside me.

Public is a generous term for the street. No one would come running to help if I screamed. But it's better than letting him follow me home. A whole lot better.

"Relax," he says, somewhat dry and almost sad. "If I wanted to fuck you, I'd have met you in the club."

And if he'd wanted to kill me, he could have done it a hundred times by now. He'd followed me here. I'm still alive. But I can't relax. Not while I'm wondering whether he followed me any other night and what he saw. Who he saw. "Plenty of guys would like a freebie."

Has he followed me home? I have to assume he hasn't. I have to believe she's safe, otherwise there's no point to any of this.

"I'll always pay," he says, and I know he's teasing a little. But a little bit not. "Cross my heart."

It's more than money now. It's also distance. He's drawing a line in the sand. He's telling me he needs that line just as much as I do. "And tip," I add. Because I can tease too.

His smile always dawns like the morning, slow and warm, wiping away the night's chill. "Not *just* the tip, though."

Oh my God. I roll my eyes, but I'm smiling too. "So what did you want to talk about?"

"Lots of things," he says, catching my hand. "Like who you're afraid of."

I flinch. I'm afraid of Byron. I'm afraid of my father. I'm afraid of everyone. "What makes you think I'm afraid?"

"I know a girl in trouble when I see one. And you're it."

"So you're here to save the day?" More likely he'd get himself killed. Yeah, the man is obviously tough—but my father has a fucking army at his command. Kip should find some other girl to stalk and harass. A different one to use. He should find a different girl to protect. "I can't be what you want."

A grim smile flickers over his face. "You really don't know what I want, sweetheart. You'd be a lot more scared if you did."

❖   ❖   ❖

Six months ago

I'M STILL FACEDOWN on the desk, being pounded, when I hear the door open. I tense. What if it's a guest? But then I hear the cadence of my father's gait—one light step, one heavy, one creak of his cane.

Oh God. I pray that he leaves.

Byron doesn't stop fucking me. His thrusts don't change at all, not faster or slower. He fucks me like he has forever—and he does. My father can't stop him. My father *won't* stop him.

One light, one heavy, one creak of his cane. My father's

coming closer.

He must see me by now, must know what's happening. And yet he keeps walking nearer to us. He rounds the desk. *Light, heavy, creak.*

And stops.

"Sir?" Byron's breathing is heavy, the word clipped short. It's a parody of respect, the word *sir,* as he fucks the man's daughter over his desk. As his cock invades me, splitting me open.

"Byron." My father sounds tired and impossibly old. "Our documents. Look at them."

The documents are crushed in my hands. They are smeared with my mascara that smears across my cheek. They are ruined.

"Almost done," Byron says on a grunt.

I shiver from disgust, that my father is here watching this, that my fiancé doesn't seem to mind. I am something worse than a future wife or a beloved daughter. I am a pet, forced to beg and roll over for my dinner. And it's not even disgust at my father or at Byron that hollows out my stomach—it's disgust for myself. I let them do this to me. I don't fight. I can't fight. It's not only me who'll get hurt if I do.

A hand hovers over my head, shaking, trembling. Not Byron's hand. It's my father's.

He always shakes now. The doctors say it will only get worse. It started in his hand, then moved to his legs. That's when he started using the cane. He would have lost his life too. In his business any sign of weakness can be fatal. Competitors move in, take over. But no one came to kill my father because Byron stepped in.

With my father's blessing, he'll take control of the family's businesses. His marriage to me will solidify the deal in the eyes of the more traditional mafiosos, smooth the way so less people fight it. And my father will get to live out his life in the empire he built, safe and sound and stroking the hair of his daughter as she gets fucked over his desk.

Every cell in my body revolts against his touch. But I remain still and outwardly calm. It's a skill I learned early in life—facing a monster and showing no fear.

I'm surrounded by monsters.

Byron grunts and digs his fingers into my flesh. He pulses inside me, and I know he's coming. *Finally.*

He pulls out with a wet sound. A warm swipe against my ass cheek quickly cools as he wipes his dick dry on me. The sound of a zipper fills the quiet room, then rustling as he puts himself to rights. My dress flips down.

As I lift my face, a piece of paper flutters back to the desk, unstuck from my cheek. My father strokes my hair one last time, and then his hand falls away. It feels like a strange ceremony has just taken place, the weight of it heavy in the air. The way a regular father would hand his daughter to her new husband at her wedding. But my father isn't normal. He's a Mafia don. The last in the line of the prestigious Moretti family. And he's given his blessing to the union.

I stand and catch myself on the desk before I fall. My

legs are weak, like a baby deer struggling to hold myself up. It's Byron who pushes me up with a soft pat on my ass.

My father doesn't meet my eyes. Instead he busies himself straightening the papers on the desk.

Byron sits and gives me a bland smile. You'd never think he was inside me one minute ago. "Go back to the party. We have business to discuss." He pauses, then adds, "Enjoy yourself, darling."

We aren't in love. I hate him, and I think he might hate me too—for being born into the right family. Just with the wrong gender. If I'd been a man, I would have taken over the business in my own right. As it is, the other families require a man to lead, to respect. It's not only my cunt that keeps me docile, though. I don't have the heart to fight, to lead, to *kill* like they do.

Like Byron does. I'm terrified of him, but we'll be married in a matter of months.

CHAPTER SIX

KIP PREPARES MY coffee.

Of all the things that have happened in my life over the past twelve months, over the past twenty years, this is the thing I find strangest. He not only orders my coffee, but when it becomes clear I am not moving to take it, he pulls the little packet to his side. I've never been served, never been helped by people who weren't paid to do it. Never been helped by anyone who didn't have something to gain. So what is he after?

"Cream?" he asks.

I nod my head, and he tears the lid off the little cup of nondairy creamer. We're sitting at a corner booth in a crappy diner. Everything is dirty here, including me. But not him. He's not exactly clean either. He's something else. Something dark and serious and solemn. His hands mesmerize me, so large and strong and yet careful. He's stone, rough-edged and impenetrable. And I am air, already blowing away.

"Sugar?"

My nod is surer this time, quicker, because I want to see him do this.

He doesn't disappoint. Broad, square-tipped fingers

rip open a single blue packet. He pours sugar into the black liquid and stirs. He gives me this, when all the other men just take and take.

I have experience with big, strong men. Careful ones too. I know they are the worst kind. But somehow I don't think he'll hurt me. Maybe that's just wishful thinking. Maybe he's a mirage. I could open my eyes and find myself in the middle of a desert, dying of thirst. But that's where I've been. Even if he's an illusion, it can't hurt worse than the truth.

I wrap my hands around the ceramic, trying to soak up the warmth.

As if he notices, as if he *cares,* he says, "Want my jacket?"

"No." Every kind thing he does makes me want him more. And makes me push him farther away.

Weary amusement flickers over his coarse features. "I appreciate you coming here with me."

"You didn't give me much of a choice."

"No." He sobers. "No, I didn't. And I imagine you've had your fill of men pushing you around."

I shift on the hard plastic cushion. I've been pushed around in the literal sense. Does he know that? Is it possible he knows where I'm running from—*who* I'm running from? But the more likely answer is he means the men at the strip club. "I can take care of myself."

"I don't doubt that." There's a pause while he seems to be debating how much to tell me. "I've been watching you."

How much do you know? "Is that supposed to be a compliment?"

He leans forward, resting his elbows on his knees, gaze intent on mine. "I'm not planning to hurt you. I just want to get to know you."

My chest tightens. "Where I come from, that's the same thing."

His eyes darken. "But you can take care of yourself," he says, the words a challenge.

The smile that comes out is more a baring of teeth. It's either that or cry. "I'm gone, aren't I? And I'm never going back."

He's not impressed. "You're dancing in a strip club and walking down the worst street in Tanglewood. You have no defenses. You have *nothing* to protect yourself."

I flinch. "Is this how you get to know someone? By insulting them?"

Regret passes over his face. "No. I'm an asshole. I just meant maybe you don't have it all figured out. And that maybe I could help."

"No one can help me." No one goes up against the Moretti family and lives.

Which is why I know that one day they'll find me. And kill me. As long as they don't touch Clara, I'm okay with that. That's enough. It has to be.

"Maybe not," he says, "but I have a confession to make. I do want to help you. But I also need your help."

My laugh comes out unsteady, almost breathy. Afraid. "I bet you do. I bet you have a very big, very serious problem that I could smooth right out for you. Soften you up."

He doesn't crack a smile. "Honey," he says with warning.

But it sounds ridiculous. The name is ridiculous. His low, serious voice just makes it worse.

I laugh then, for real. I think this is the funniest thing I've heard in days, or weeks. Or months. It's the funniest thing I've ever heard, this fake name and fake smile and fake relationship I can't have. And help? That's not real either. That's a story he's telling, whether he knows it or not. You know what's real? Sex. That's all I have to offer him.

I might become a little unhinged as I sit there laughing. I expect him to get all serious and angry, but then something crazy happens. He starts laughing too. First it's just a quirk of his lips and a soft exhale of breath. But then he chuckles alongside me, shaking his head.

His smile fades. "You don't belong in that place."

I suck in a sharp breath. "And why's that? My tits aren't big enough? I don't use the right songs?"

"You keep thinking it's not going to hurt," he says gently. "The dancing. The fucking. You're still surprised when it does."

Pain is a wide chasm in my gut. "What do you know about dancing?"

"Not much," he admits. "Just what I see. I see you expecting the best from the men that come through there. It's a kind of suicide, sweetheart. It hurts just to watch you."

"You're wrong." Anger is cold as ice, numbing all the other feelings. "I'm exactly right for this job. Because I don't give a fuck."

His smile is sad. "Then tell me your name."

My lips tighten. "Never."

He nods once. "I'll see you on Saturday, Honey."

"And I'll suck you off," I warn, though it's the strangest warning I've ever given. "That's all."

"We'll see." He drops a twenty on the table and stands to leave. "Take care of yourself until then. This isn't a safe part of the city."

WATERY DAYLIGHT BREAKS over the city just as I reach the extended-stay motel.

Not quite as run-down, not quite as terrifying as Candy's building, but still depressing. Red brick faded to pink. Iron bars on the windows. Palm trees in the courtyard do little to make the place more tropical or cheery. Neither do the Christmas lights wrapped around them. It's a colorful prison.

Heavy curtains in my room's window block my view inside. I pull out the key card and slip it into the reader, already looking forward to a long day's sleep to help me forget what I did at night. *Clara.* The name is on the tip of my tongue, ready to call out in greeting. But some deep-seated instinct keeps me cautious.

I struggle with the heavy duffel bag that has my work

clothes and shoes. The heavy door is like a rat trap, trying to snap closed, jarring my shoulder in the process.

The motel room is dark.

And the little Madonna statuette stands in the window.

It's a figurine made of thin plastic, with a white cord attached. It's designed to light up, but the lightbulb inside has long since died. It was actually in the motel room when we got there. Clara fished it out of the trash and put it on the window. She claimed it would protect us. And it has. It's our way of signaling that something is wrong. If we're ever found out, if the room is compromised and one of us is forced to run, we'll take the Madonna out of the window. It's a relief to see it each night, standing small and gaudy and proud in front of the drapes.

I am cautious, looking left and right before using the key card. I am always cautious, because if someone tracked me here and really wanted to hurt me, I'd be screwed. My only saving grace today was that Kip hadn't tracked me all the way home. And that he hadn't wanted to hurt me.

No, he just wants to fuck you.

All the lights are off, even the bathroom. "Clara," I whisper.

No answer. I step farther into the room, and my eyes slowly adjust. I can make out the two beds and the table in the corner. And a dark bundle in the center of one bed, almost hidden in the shadows. I cross the room and gently shake her shoulder.

Clara blinks up at me. "Honor?"

"I'm here."

"Oh thank God. I was so worried about you. You were late. Are you okay?"

"I'm fine." My voice comes out too sharp, so I try to soften it. "I'm fine, but you remember what we talked about. If there's trouble, I won't bring it back to the room. You have the stash of money and—"

"I'm not leaving without you," she says fiercely.

Worry tightens my gut. If anything goes wrong at the strip club, if I don't come back when I'm supposed to, Clara is supposed to run. Without me. But she never quite agrees to it. Sometimes she is silent while I detail the escape routes. Other times she tells me no.

I extend my hand, and she lets me pull her up. I don't let go, instead hugging her close and breathing deep. We may not agree on everything, but I love her. She's my sister, and I'll never let anything happen to her. She squeezes me back, tight enough to steal my breath.

Her voice is small. "I thought you might not come back."

It's easy to forget that she's only sixteen. She's been brave through this whole thing, but she's still a kid. She should be worrying about pop quizzes and who asks her to homecoming.

Not living in a broken-down motel, afraid of a man at the door.

My throat feels too tight to answer. But she's counting on me to be strong, so I am. She's the only thing keeping me together. The urge for us to run now rises up in me. Kip's questions hit too close to home. He knows something more than he's telling me, but it could just as easily be about the club than my past. And Ivan… well, now he's telling me not to leave. It's a shit time for him to take an interest.

We'll stay, for now. "Remember, Clara. If I don't come back twenty-four hours after I should, you need to go. Don't ask questions. And don't wait for me."

She looks down. It's not agreement, but it's all I can get for now.

I change the subject. "Did you do your lessons today?"

She can't go to high school, and obviously we don't have the tutors from home, but I still insist she does her high school course work. I'm determined that she's going to at least have the knowledge, even if she won't have the diploma with her name on it. One day in the future, the dust will settle.

One day she'll be able to live a regular life. I have to believe that, or all of this is for nothing. Every baring of my breasts, every touch of a stranger—for nothing.

I see you expecting the best from the men that come through there. It's a kind of suicide, sweetheart.

"Of course. It was easy." Clara switches on a lamp, sending a weak glow over the tattered bedspread and furniture.

"Give it to me. I'll check it."

She rolls her eyes and hands over the workbooks. "Yes, Mom."

I freeze, remembering the dark-haired, dark-eyed woman who was our mother. The woman Clara barely knew. A deep longing rends my chest. I know she couldn't have helped us through this. In some ways it's her fault we're in this mess. But I still miss her.

Clara looks stricken. "I'm sorry. I shouldn't have said that."

Her cheeks are still gently rounded, as are her arms. I grew up like a beanpole, growing breasts late. They're still small for a stripper. But Clara was always a bundle of joyful, chubby girl. She's gotten slimmer as she grows into a teenager, her waist tightening, her curves turning womanly. But her eyes still sparkle like a child's. Eventually her baby fat will fall away. She will no longer curl up like a child when she sleeps. But I want that sparkle to stay.

I'll do anything to keep it. I already have.

"It's okay," I say softly. "I'm just sorry you didn't get to know her longer."

She takes my hand. "I am too. But I couldn't ask for a better big sister."

"God, you're sweet." And it strikes me then, with the force of an explosion, how similar she is to Kip. How *open* they both are. Maybe that's why I seem to trust Kip, even when I clearly shouldn't. Maybe that's why I don't want him to die.

Her smile is like his too—sad. "I love you."

My hand tightens around hers like a vise. I can't say it back. Haven't been able to say the word *love* since the day I heard my mother cry out for the last time. There are too many other words crowding it out. Words like *run* and *hide* and *don't let them touch you.*

And the biggest word of all, floating right at the surface, struggling to break free. *Help.*

CHAPTER SEVEN

T HE FIRST THING I see when I walk into the dressing room is Candy's glossy blonde hair. Relief courses through me, more than I'd even expected. It's dangerous, that relief. I shouldn't be forming attachments here. I might have to leave at a moment's notice. Leaving is hard enough—covering my tracks and finding a new job that doesn't ask questions. What I don't need is to leave friends behind. Candy is a coworker. Practically a stranger.

Still, my chest feels tight when I see her safe and sound. "I was worried about you," I blurt out before I can stop it.

She turns, and I can see the shadow around one eye and the puffiness of her lower lip. I can see the tension in the fake smile she gives me. She isn't safe after all, isn't sound.

"You shouldn't have," she says. "Just partying too hard. Having too much fun."

I reach for her mouth, pulling back when she flinch-es. "That doesn't look like fun," I say softly.

Her gaze drops. "Things got out of hand."

Things have a way of doing that. I drop to my knees,

kneeling in front of her, hoping she'll see me. Really see me. "Candy. Is there anything I can do? Can I help?"

Her throat moves as she swallows. "You have your own shit to deal with."

And my sister comes first. Of course she does. If there's only room for one person on the raft, I'd give it to Clara. I'm already doing that. But I can't look away when I see Candy like this, bruised and afraid. I've been there. "Is it a boyfriend? Can you leave him?"

That makes her smile for real. "Like you?"

My breath squeezes out of me. "Sometimes it's better than staying."

"Out of the frying pan, into the fire. Do you think you're safe here? I don't know where you came from, but this can't be much better."

I shiver, hearing the echo of Kip's words in hers. *How about because you're not safe there? None of you are.* Candy and I may not be safe, but no one is touching my sister. No one is making her eye dark and her lip puffy. That's a hell of a lot better.

"Maybe you should tell Ivan," I say, standing.

She laughs. "He'll like it too much."

My stomach turns over. "He's not that bad."

"He's soft on you. You're made of glass. He knows that. They all know that."

Anger rises up in me. "I'm not fragile."

I'm not exactly strong either—something better than that. I'm already torn apart, already in pieces. There's nothing left to break.

She stands then too, bringing us chest to chest. A challenging glint enters her pretty blue eyes. "Aren't you? Coming in here, trying to *help* me, like we're besties or something. Showing up at my place because you're worried I'm OD'ing."

Her words are like a harsh gust of wind, stealing my breath and pushing me back a step. "How did you—"

"I know some of those guys on the steps." Her eyebrows rise. "I've fucked some of them. They told me a girl with black hair and small tits and the greenest eyes they ever saw—like money, they said—came and knocked on my door."

"You could have been OD'ing," I say with disgust—at myself. "You could have been getting a beating. And I left you there."

"As opposed to what, camping outside my door?" She scoffs. "And anyway, the assholes on the stairs *let* you leave. Because you're like a goddamn Mother Theresa, and even those hardened assholes didn't want to touch your pale, innocent skin."

"Why are you pissed that I was worried about you? Is it so bad that someone cares?"

"Yes, it is so fucking bad. It's a death sentence around here, so cut that shit out."

Realization settles over me. "Oh. You're worried about me."

She scowls. "I couldn't care less about you. I was dancing before you got here, and I'll be dancing when you're gone. You're a goddamn chime of the clock."

I can't really help the smile that spreads across my face. "You really care."

"I really, really don't."

"Can we braid each other's hair and tell ghost stories?" I tease.

An exasperated look crosses over her face, so vehement, so *desperate* that I think she might actually hit me. That's how much she doesn't want to care about me. How much she wants to stay detached, just like I did. But we can't quite do it. Maybe that is a death sentence, but if it is, we're already dead.

She glances to the door—empty—and then back at me. Her voice is quiet and, this time, sincere. She isn't trying to pretend we don't care. She's telling me that she does. "You might be safe in my apartment. People know me there. But not on the street. Not wandering around alone. And if you got caught there, who would take care of whoever it is you're hiding."

My eyes widen, because I may have formed attachments at work, but I've *never* confided about Clara. She's never been to the club, and she'll never come here. "I don't know what you're talking about."

"I've seen you take food from the kitchen at the end of the day. And since you're thin as a beanpole, I figured you weren't chowing down while watching infomercials."

I shut my eyes. "Has anyone else—"

"Not that I know of. Even Lola doesn't suspect. I'd know if she did because we talk about you."

Despite my distress, my lips lift in a faint smile. "Gee, thanks."

"It's because we do care," she whispers. "And we don't want you to die."

✧   ✧   ✧

I'M BLINDED EVERY time I go onstage, but this time is different. Because even though I can't see, I know Kip is there. I can feel him watching me, wanting me, *counting on me*. When I am onstage, it's impossible to hide. I'm exposed. And I have to face the pain in my chest, the one I feel because I'm bound to let him down.

I dance with sure feet and strong hips. I dance like this will be my last time onstage. I dance for *him*.

Even though I pretend not to see him near the front. For a man undercover, he isn't hiding. He isn't slinking near the edges, in the shadows, hoping not to be seen. He's in plain sight—like me. We have that in common. It binds us together when I'd rather forget.

Blue finds me after my dance, when I would have gone onto the floor to make the rounds. He grabs me when I try to move past him. "What happened to Candy?" he demands.

I blink, taken aback. Sometimes he seems to almost care about us girls. Although maybe he's just angry at damaged goods. And his fingers dig into my arm. "I don't know. She didn't tell me."

"She talks to you."

"Well, not about that."

He blows out a breath and looks to the side. His hand falls away. "Is it the same place Lola's gone?"

I didn't even know Lola had left. If we are soldiers, we are falling one by one. What are we defending? I have Clara. I don't know what Lola or Candy has. "I thought she wasn't working today."

"Only because she called and took herself off rotation. It's not like her to miss a Saturday, though. Not when Ivan—" He stops abruptly, lips firming. He's said too much, which is strange enough. But I can feel his distress, which is stranger still.

His concern feels like water tugging at my feet, an undertow. It's swirling beneath the surface, waiting to suck me down. There's a current in this club. I can't see it, but I can feel it.

"Lola can take care of herself," I say because it's true. Between the three of us, Lola is the tough one. The take-no-prisoners one. Men need to look out when she prowls through the floor, not the other way around.

"Yeah, right," he mutters. "Just like Candy and you."

I flinch. "We do our job. That's all you pay us to do."

His grin is dark and unpleasant. "And I do my job, which is to keep you ladies pretty and available."

It's almost soothing to hear his crude words, having the Blue I know and loathe back. He's an asshole, and I wouldn't know how to deal with him otherwise. "I'm available. For those who pay." I raise my eyebrows to let him know that he hasn't. Not ever.

Not for any of the girls, as far as I know.

His eyes darken as he looks me up and down, taking my measure. He's had his hands on every girl in this club, if only to rough us up or move us around. We are dolls to him, and he's the one pulling strings. There is lust in his eyes, and a threat. But his heart's not in it.

The startling thing is to realize he has a heart after all.

"Look, if you want to keep us pretty, check on Candy. Someone's hurting her."

"No shit," he snaps. "She looks like a fucking evidence photo. How am I supposed to put her on the floor?"

Charming. "If you don't know who's messing with her, tell Ivan. He'll get it out of her."

"I bet he will," he mutters in a tone that means exactly what Candy had said. *He'd like it too much.* "Maybe I should tell him about you."

My heart thuds. Does he mean Kip? Ivan must have told him I'm supposed to stay away. So why hasn't Blue told on me yet? What does he want from me—a bribe? "What do you want?"

His gaze sharpens. "I want you to do your fucking job."

It's hard to speak. "I'm doing it."

"And watch your back."

My chest feels tight. "I always do."

He sighs, shaking his head.

He doesn't believe me—or maybe he just knows it's a hopeless cause. I can watch my back. I can watch as the tiger gets closer. I can watch as he leaps. And there won't be a damn thing I can do to stop him.

"I know that guy," he says. "When you've been in the game as long as I have, you get to know who the players are."

"What game is that?"

A smile then. "The killing game."

CHAPTER EIGHT

THE CLUB DOESN'T have any windows, but I know it's been raining. The customers clothes are wet—especially the tops of their shirts and the hems of their pants. They hustle inside and then linger over empty glasses, reluctant to get rained on again. That would be good for business, except that a bunch of horny guys who would've come in have decided to stay home. It's dead here.

I finish my dances and make the rounds with minimal fanfare. When it's time to go home, I'm exhausted, my mind numb. I wrap my jacket tightly around me as I step outside.

There's only a light drizzle, though the hours of stormy weather have left their mark. All the surfaces are slick, from the brick walls to the metal lampposts. Puddles stretch over the sidewalk, almost touching. I pick my way through them. My feet are already aching. The last thing I need is a shoe full of freezing water.

I'm so focused on the ground that I almost don't see anyone there.

A shadow detaches from the wall.

I only have time to gasp and clutch the duffel bag to

my body like a shield. Then a hand is on my arm, tugging me in, dragging me into the alley.

My shout is muffled by the hand that is over my mouth.

I'm pressed with my back to the cool brick, a hard body in front of me, unmovable—trapped. It's pitch-black in the alley, with only our harsh breaths mingling, communicating before we've said a word.

His head lowers. I can't even see the shadow, the shape of it. I can only feel him coming closer.

Warm lips press against my temple. It feels almost chaste, except that he's holding me up against a wall, pressing his whole body into me, thick and hard against my hip.

I shiver.

"Easy," a low voice says in the darkness.

Kip. Relief fills me even though it shouldn't. I can't trust him. He's speaking to me like I'm an animal, a horse he has to gentle so I don't rear up.

And maybe that's all I am, because my instinct is to fight.

He removes his hand from my mouth, and I hiss, "What are you doing?"

I hate that my voice comes out wobbly.

"Waiting for you."

That's what I was afraid of. But if he wants to hurt me, he'll have to try harder than that. I'll make him fight for it. *The killing game.* I don't even know what that means. I just know I can't trust him. "Get away from me."

I don't expect him to listen—but he does. He steps back. Just enough that the streetlamp outlines his height, his shoulders. I still can't see his expression. He is only a shadow, a deep voice. Only a question. "Who were you afraid of?"

You. "Men who drag me into alleyways."

"I'm not going to hurt you. Only talk."

"Is that why you kissed me?"

"That wasn't intentional. You smelled so fucking good."

"I smell like I've been dancing onstage for hours. Which I have been."

He leans close, breathing in at my temple. Inhaling me. "So fucking good."

That shouldn't be a compliment, not when he's acting like a caveman, but God, that makes it better. More primal. More real. "Right, well, I'm a stripper in a shitty neighborhood. It can give a girl a complex."

He glances to the street like he's never seen it before. "Get attacked often, do you?"

"Not often. I'm careful." Except for not seeing him at all. He's like a lion hiding in the tall grass. Only in this case they're tall buildings of steel and concrete. By the time the gazelle sees him, it's too late.

"Then why do you work here?" he asks.

I roll my eyes. "Let's not do this."

"Do what?" He looks so damn innocent, his eyes a touch too wide. He knows exactly what I'm talking about.

"The rescue game."

"The rescue game," he repeats.

"You know, where you ask about my problem as if you care."

"I do actually care, though." His lips curve. "A little."

That makes me snort. "And then you offer to help me out. You can spot me a hundred for my light bill. Or hey, here's an even better idea: I can go live with you rent-free. All I have to do is fuck you every night."

"Ouch."

"And then leave when you get tired of me."

He is silent a moment. "Wow, you really think I'm a bastard."

Something in my chest twists. I could have just let him say his piece. It probably would have been the same shit that every stripper has heard before, but I didn't give him much of a chance, did I? "I'm sorry. I shouldn't have—"

"No, I mean, you're right."

"Really?" It doesn't surprise me that I'm right. It surprises me that he'll admit it.

"I am a bastard," he says. "Bastard enough to charge you your share of rent, that's for sure. And we're trading off on doing the dishes."

A smile tugs at my lips. "Too soon?"

"A little. I could spot you a twenty. We'll work up from there."

I roll my eyes. "Okay, so maybe I jumped to conclusions."

He stops, dead serious. "No, you're right to call me on my bullshit. Even if that wasn't exactly what I want from you."

"So what is it that you want from me?"

He is quiet. "To walk you home. Can I? Tomorrow."

It's the sweetest thing I've ever been asked. Like holding my hand, like a kiss on the cheek. I'm lonely enough that it seems impossible, and I stare disbelieving at the oasis. Maybe a part of me liked it dry. "And today?"

"Today..." He slides a hand down my hip, hitching me up between the wall and his body. "Today we can play a game."

"Not the rescue game," I whisper.

He runs his tongue down my neck while his hand reaches under me, lifting me higher, until my feet are off the ground. "Don't count on me to rescue you, Honey. I'd only disappoint."

But he won't disappoint me in this. That's the unspoken promise as his fingers find my pussy and rub through my yoga pants—hard and fast. My moan is caught in his mouth, his lips flush against mine, his tongue seeking and rough.

"What's the game then?" I ask, shuddering as he nips my shoulder.

"The game is whoever comes first...loses."

My laugh turns into a gasp as the rigid length of him presses flush against my clit, our clothes made of air and whimsy—nothing at all. We rock this way, in time to that ancient rhythm, feeling the beat of our hearts and our sex. There's a beat coming from the other side of the wall, the music of someone onstage, the sound of someone's defilement, and we use it, make it our own, writhing against each other until we reach a fever pitch.

Then abruptly, I'm back on the ground.

I would fall except for his hands steadying me, turning me around.

I'm facing the wall now, almost hugging it, face and breasts against brick. And my ass exposed as he yanks down my pants, pushing them to my knees. Coarse hands position my hips, pushing me out further so he can see... so he can penetrate.

There's a rip. And a tear. And a blunt nudge at my sex.

I've fucked his fingers and his boot. But this is the first time he's put his cock in me. It's fitting that I'm not looking at him. Both cold and hot as I press against the cool, gritty surface and get invaded from behind.

He's so thick, and I whimper. "Almost there," he mutters.

But if I thought he'd take mercy, go slower, I'd be wrong. He presses all the way deep, tilting my pelvis to take him all the way inside. My mouth opens on a silent gasp. I'm too full like this. Too full of his cock. Too full of memories.

This is how Byron fucked me, from behind.

But it's completely different too. Completely hot.

Completely amazing as he fills me, again and again. As his hand reaches around to play with my clit. Casually, as if we have all the time in the world. There's no rush, even with us out in the open.

He can fuck me forever—and he does, sliding into me until I'm slick and swollen, until my clit is plump and needy against his fingers, begging for relief.

My moan has all my pent up need. To be held and fucked. To be wanted.

"Come, Honey," he whispers in my ear. "Come on my cock. I want to feel you gush."

And I can't hold back—not my body's responses, not my tears. I shudder through climax, clamping down hard, feeling wet heat spill over his cock and down my legs. I lose the game, but it doesn't feel like losing, not with molten pleasure filling my body. Then he's gripping my hips like steel, digging into the soft flesh, using my body like a torque, thrusting up into me as he climaxes with a growl.

✧   ✧   ✧

BYRON IS SUPPOSED to be the dangerous one. My father. Even Ivan. They are like winds that blow me, pushing me onward like I weigh nothing. Even when I dig my heels in, the rock face is slippery with pebbles and I can't find my balance. I'm afraid of the wind, afraid of its force, but what I didn't realize is that the greater danger lay ahead of me. Kip is my cliff. Every gust of wind pushes me closer.

It's only a matter of time before I fall.

Kip is waiting outside when I leave the club. I breathe a sigh of relief. Each time I think I must have scared him away. He doesn't come inside the club anymore. I envy him that.

"Is this going to become a regular thing with you?" I ask.

The streetlight a few feet away draws more shadows than it hides. His eyes are dark, unfathomable. But the quirk of his lips, it tells me all I need to know. "I have something for you."

"Really?" This interests me more than it should. I start walking, and he steps beside me easily. Just like that he's walking me home, as if we're in high school. As if either of us were innocent teenagers.

I don't know what it would have felt like to do this. For one thing, I never went to school. I had tutors and books. I had locks on my doors. And for another thing, I've never been innocent. I've always known about the world I lived in, the violence it contained.

He reaches into his back pocket, and part of me, that corner reserved for fight-or-flight, tenses. What if he pulls something awful out? It's not like I really know him well.

Then he reaches out, palm up, with something small and cylindrical on his hand. "For you," he says.

I take it, examining the smooth silver casing. And the trigger. "What is this?"

His expression grows somber. "I figured since you are

experienced with men jumping out of alleyways, you should have something to protect you. It's a Taser."

A Taser? I ran away from violence. I don't want more of it. Even to protect myself, I'm not sure I could hurt someone else. How do you choose your life over someone else's? Not that a Taser would kill someone.

At least, I think it wouldn't.

"Careful," he says, his hand covering mine.

Maybe he saw my fingers going loose, almost dropping the Taser. I freeze at the feel of him, the warmth. The gentleness. It's almost as jarring as seeing him come out of the shadows.

"Like this," he says. "This is the safety switch. Right now it's on. When you want to use this, you'll flip it and then press this here."

His fingers manipulate mine as he shows me how I'd use this. Hypothetically. It's a good thing his hand is around mine because my hand is shaking. I might tase myself, which would be too painfully symbolic—as well as actually painful.

"This will hurt," I say, like a question. Even though I know the answer.

"It will incapacitate someone," he says, letting go. "Long enough for you to get away."

I run my finger along the smooth metal case. It's still warm from his body. "Will it hurt them?"

He smiles a little. "Oh, it'll fucking hurt. Doesn't matter how big he is, he'll go down. But if you mean long-term injuries, no. You're very concerned about this hypothetical guy. He would have been hurting you if you use this. Why do you care what happens to him?"

"I just do."

He studies me. "If someone bothers you, don't hesitate."

I take his measure, imagining what it would be like to use this on him. It feels impossible, but that doesn't matter. Just the idea that he got this for me makes me feel warmer, stronger. "So I could use this on you?"

"That depends," he says. "Am I bothering you?"

He has a certain elemental quality in that dark T-shirt hugging his abs, the black leather jacket molded around his arms. The buttery denim encasing his legs. Like a panther. But that is a disguise, as much as the stilettos and tear-away bra I use onstage. It's a flashy kind of sexiness, designed to distract.

Beneath that smile and those muscles is an intelligence I should be wary of. A watchfulness. He knows exactly what to say to get under my defenses. He knows exactly what to give me, in the form of this small weapon, to make me give in.

"No." Pinpricks batter my eyes. I blink quickly. "Thank you."

A slight lift of one large shoulder. "It's nothing."

"No," I say, too loud. I try to lower my voice, but I know it's still betraying me. "I'm serious—thank you. This is one of the nicest things…"

I can't talk. I couldn't explain it even if I could. Men have always wanted to use me, to hurt me. He is the only one who wants to protect me.

He doesn't move much, but his energy shifts, withdraws. He becomes almost bashful. His voice is gruff when he says, "Honey, if that's true, you need to meet nicer guys."

My laugh comes out watery. I got expensive jewelry from Byron, but that was about him, about dressing me up like a doll. Kip gave me something thoughtful, something to help me feel safe. I've only felt this way once, but it's already addictive. I want to tell him something else I'm afraid of, just like he keeps asking me to, and watch him fix it for me.

There's a reason I don't do drugs like Candy, though. I can't afford to be dependent.

"You're more than enough for me," I tell him. More than I can handle, actually. I take his hand and tug him toward the alley he must have been waiting in.

He follows me two steps and then pulls me back to him. "Sweetheart?"

The word shudders through me. That's addictive too.

"I want to thank you properly," I tell him.

But he drops my hand. "That's not necessary."

Now he sounds pissed, like he's clenching his teeth. A muscle in his jaw flexes.

What did I do wrong? I know he wants me. I put my palm on his chest and feel his heart steady underneath. Trailing lower, I feel the bulge in his jeans. Oh yeah, he wants me.

He steps back. "I'm leaving now. And next time you see me, you should use what I gave you."

Then he is gone, merging back into the shadows, disappearing the same way that he came.

CHAPTER NINE

Six months ago

THERE IS A space between the walls of the office and the hallway. I don't know if it was some flaw in the original architectural plans or the result of shoddy workmanship. Or maybe the gap is intentional, a barrier between the ugliness that happens inside this room and the family living space. But I learned as a child that I could fit my body into that space and eavesdrop. Even though I have grown into a woman, I can still fit, my breasts and ass pushed flat against the dusty inner walls.

That's where I go when I leave my father and Byron in the office. Something about the way they spoke, the energy in the air, told me it was going to be important. So I hide and listen.

Byron's voice is soft but firm. "We need to announce it. Tonight."

"So soon?" My father's voice is a sharp contrast, faint and rasping. So unlike the man I looked up to for so long, the man who could command mercenaries and criminals. Now he suffers every time he takes a breath.

I'm not even sorry.

"This will give us time to make arrangements."

"She hasn't even been told," my father says.

I stiffen where I'm crouched. What haven't they told me?

"Telling her was your job," Byron says sharply. "She's your daughter."

My mind races, flashing disturbing images behind my eyes, a terrifying slideshow of all the things they could do to me—all the things my father wouldn't want to say.

Furniture scrapes over hardwood. "It doesn't matter if she knows," Byron continues. "She'll find out with everyone. And she'll be thrilled. A governor's son? He's a bigger catch than I am."

Ice floods my veins. Oh no. This is so much worse. Because they aren't talking about me. They're talking about Clara.

"I'm not sure about the match," my father murmurs. I have to strain to hear him. "Those reports, in the newspaper…"

"Exaggerations," Byron says smoothly. Always smooth.

A pause. "There were pictures."

My heart beats faster. My father never speaks to Byron this way, becoming more meek as he grows sicker. As Byron takes over.

"Pictures can be faked. You know that as well as I do. Evidence only says what it's meant to." Even from here I can hear the undercurrent of warning in Byron's voice. My father is at his mercy, he means. Byron is the one in charge now, despite the deference he still shows my father in public.

There is more murmuring. Then the clap of a fist on a solid wood desk.

"Don't worry so much," Byron says in an easy tone. "The governor and I go way back. Pledged to the same frat, a few years apart."

"It's not only Clara I worry for," my father says. "Honor. There are marks…"

Oh God. He's really bringing them up? He's really *seen* them? I shudder, running my hands over my arms. There are goose bumps there. This is too strange a conversation to hear. I wish I'd walked away.

I've never been sure whether my father has noticed the bruises. On the worst days Byron would lock me in my room. A cell-phone photo taken by a maid and sold to the tabloid could derail his political ambitions, after all. I guess I'd assumed my father was too distracted— too much in pain—to notice the smaller marks Byron left. It almost hurts worse to know he saw them but did nothing.

Even if he's standing up to Byron now.

"She doesn't concern you any longer," Byron says softly. "She's my fiancée. Soon she'll be my wife. Whatever we do behind closed doors is my business."

"Yes…yes, of course. But Honor is a woman now. And Clara is still just sixteen."

"Honor is mine to take care of. Clara too, by exten-sion. I'll watch over them when you're gone."

Now the threat is explicit, potent in the air. Even through inches of cherry wood paneling I can feel it. I wait, holding my breath, to see if my father will stand up for his younger daughter the way he didn't for me.

"Besides," Byron says, his tone lethal, "Clara isn't even yours."

I flinch. The idea doesn't come as a surprise—everyone in the house, everyone in the extended family, must know the truth. But I've never heard anyone speak it before. And instead of growing angry, that seems to win my father over. Or at least wear him down.

"She would only have to date him now," my father finally says. "A governor's son. Great connections. Clara will be happy. And Honor too."

✧   ✧   ✧

ANYTHING YOU DO with other people ends up being a performance. I learned to smile the right way, to walk the right way. The way my father wanted me to.

Like many six year olds, I had an obsession with ballet. But unlike other six-year-olds, I wasn't placed in a classroom full of giggling children and pink ribbon. Instead a tutor was hired—a *ballerino* from the Royal Ballet in London and award-winning choreographer. There was no room for error. No room for the chubby layer of girlhood. Hours of practice every day honed my body and my mind until all I knew was how to please.

How to perform.

My father had molded me into the perfect stripper,

although he would be horrified to find that out. Or maybe he already knew. Fucking me over my father's desk, the bruises. He'd looked the other way.

"Want to grab a bite?" Lola asks as I head out the back.

I shake my head. "I'll see you tomorrow."

I don't bother telling her an excuse, something she'd know was a lie.

She looks me up and down. "Wouldn't hurt you to eat."

We're all slender here. The difference is she has curves that balance out. I trained my way through the time I would have grown breasts, and at twenty, I doubt they're going to grow. "The men seem to like me okay."

"Because you dance like a fucking ice princess. You're untouchable."

"The men seem to touch me okay too."

She smirks. "You should borrow Candy's outfit. You'd pass for thirteen."

I make a face. "Don't be like that."

"Honest?"

"Mean."

Her gaze flicks down, but I see the hurt before it does. "Same thing around here," she murmurs before turning away.

My hand reaches for her—to apologize, to tell her I'll eat with her after all. We'll find some greasy diner and spend five bucks on rubbery egg whites. It wouldn't be so bad. But I can't give up this time.

I learned long ago to keep some things to myself. So I curl my hand into a fist and push out the back door. There is only one place around here I'll find privacy. Not onstage. Not even in the motel room I share with my sister. No, my refuge is the roof of the building, behind the stairs.

Metal creaks as I climb to the top. The old fire escape isn't remotely stable, and that means I'll be left alone. Cracked concrete and debris, so different from the fine ballet floor my father had installed.

No one can see me here, and when I dance, I dance for myself.

A simple dance, without music—only the sound of my breath. *Plié. Relevés.* I dance for myself as the sun spreads over the city, yellow hands reaching building by building, until my muscles are sore and my breath comes short. I stretch my body in a grand arabesque until it becomes my own again—no longer a thing to be wrung out by other hands. I push myself now.

I make myself hurt.

If I'm too late, Clara will worry. So eventually I grab my duffel bag and head for the stairs. I climb down, yanking at the strap of my bag where it gets caught on the metal.

"Need a hand?"

I jump and almost bang my head into the railing. *That voice.* It rumbles through me, diving for every soft and vulnerable space, making me flinch. Kip.

I whirl to face him. "You scared me."

He raises an eyebrow, looking wholly unconcerned. "I wondered where you went."

My heart is still beating too fast, and I take the opportunity to examine him. He wears his usual dark T-shirt and dark jeans, with a black leather jacket. *I don't fuck around,* the clothes say. I've seen a lot of posers come through the club, but the watchful eyes and scarred hands back up his claim. This is a man who knows how to fight. This is a man who has fought before—and won.

I have no business with a man like this. I don't need another person to perform for.

"Don't," I say flatly. "Don't wonder. If I'm not in the club, I'm unavailable. If I'm not there, I don't even exist. Forget you even know me."

He smiles without humor. "I'm afraid I can't do that."

Of course he can't. Or won't. But then, I can't seem to stop thinking about him either. And not just when he'll show up again and whether he'll fuck me. Not just how much he'll pay me. No, I can't help wondering where he goes when he leaves. If there's a woman waiting for him. Hoping there's not.

Crazy.

I heft the bag high on my shoulder and push past him. "I've had a long day."

"Let me walk you home," he says. And then he plucks the bag off my shoulder without waiting for a response. "I already know where you live," he says when he sees me open my mouth. "So you're not giving anything away by letting me come."

I snort. "Right."

"I'm just walking. Making sure you get home safe. Then I'm gone."

I shouldn't believe him.

Hesitating, I wrap my arms around myself. A shudder runs through me. Sometimes I just get so damned tired of protecting myself—of protecting Clara. Of being vigilant against everything and everyone. Sometimes I wish someone would be on my side, someone I wouldn't have to protect.

"Hey," he says, his expression softening. "I'm not going to hurt you."

"Aren't you?" All my bitterness, my fiercest wish for relief comes out in the question.

His eyes widen a moment. Then he looks away.

And isn't that my answer right there? It's not even a surprise. The bile that rises in my throat is completely uncalled for. He's just like all the other men in that building.

Worse, because he makes me hope for something more.

He seems to be struggling with himself. Over how much to tell me? Over whether to hurt me? As rough and cold as he is, I can't really imagine him dragging me into the nearest alleyway and beating me. But then again, most men didn't see Byron as a monster.

The woman. The woman closest to a man can tell you what he's really like. Sometimes she's the only one who knows.

"I just want to walk you home," he says quietly, and it has the ring of truth.

And I can't fight him anymore. He's here with his tiny drops of kindness, and I am dying of thirst. "Fine. Walk me home then. But you have to tell me something about yourself. Something other people don't know about you. That's the price."

He will have to perform for me instead of the other way around.

He doesn't seem surprised. He nods and starts walking. I follow him, reluctantly curious to hear what he'll tell me. I have to admit, it's kind of nice without the strap of the bag digging into my shoulder. And it's very nice not having to watch every shadow against some unseen attacker. No one will bother me with Kip at my side.

"My mother," he says. "She sang. Professionally, for a short time. Plays and stuff, before she got knocked up and married my asshole of a father."

"Wow."

"She had a beautiful voice." He laughs softly. "Not many toddlers get sung *Madame Butterfly* for naptime. She wanted me to be better than this."

My heart clenches at the hardness in his expression, like he's holding something back. Emotion. I guess even men who fuck strippers in back rooms and then stalk them have feelings too. I don't want to care, but empathy creeps over me like the sun to the city—

unstoppable.

"I'm sorry," I say finally. Because even though I don't know the end to his story, I do. Whether that asshole father was abusive and eventually killed her or whether she just died a sad death, I know the ending isn't a happy one. I know that from the clench of his jaw and the tightness of his fists.

I swallow, thinking of my own mother. Surely she wanted better for me than this, than a stripper for a daughter. "Maybe she understands," I say, voice shaky. "Maybe she knows you're doing your best."

He looks down, and I can only see him in profile. We walk another block before he brings himself under control. "You remind me of her," he finally says.

I almost stumble even though there's no crack in the sidewalk. And I'm never clumsy. There's nothing to blame this on except pure shock. But I force myself to keep walking, head down. It may not be what I expected, but I know that from him it's the highest compliment. "Thank you."

"She had so many dreams. And no hope."

Or maybe not a compliment. And it makes me angry for him to think of her like that. To think of me like that—so many dreams and no hope. "That's not fair. She could've hoped and not told you."

He laughs. "Oh, she told me. She told me about the mansion we'd live in and about traveling the world. We lived in the fucking rubble of those dreams. We lived on them. There was damn well nothing else. Instead of enough food for dinner, we had stories. She didn't deserve that. And neither do you."

"That's not what I'm doing. I'm not waiting around for someone to come with a mansion or a plane ticket." Actually I wouldn't mind the plane ticket right about now. But I've had more than my fill of mansions and their locks and their secrets.

"Do you know how the tiger got his stripes?"

"Should I?"

"Probably not. It was in the book of stories from Kipling, the garage-sale antique." His smile is both mocking and fond.

It makes my heart ache, imagining him as a little boy—hungry and yearning. "So what is this story?"

"It's dark," he warns, "as these stories often are. The animal kingdom is a violent place."

Not so different from the human world then. "I'm not afraid."

"Aren't you?"

I don't answer.

He tips his head down, hiding his expression. "So the tiger used to be the king of the jungle. Not the lion. Back then the tiger didn't have any stripes. And he ruled with complete wisdom and mercy."

"The good old days," I say, voice wry.

He glances at me, lids half-lowered. "But one day two bucks came to him for advice, covered in blood. The tiger was taken by bloodlust and jumped on one of them, ripping out his throat."

I swallow. Not so different from the human world at all.

"And so the tiger left the jungle in shame. When he came back, the weeds and the marshes rose up and marked him with black stripes so that everyone would see what he'd done."

"If only the real world had that," I say. "Then we'd know who was bad and who wasn't."

"I think maybe it does. Look at me. Most people know on sight that I'm bad news." He's talking about the tattoos that wind their way up his forearms. And maybe also the leather jacket and the boots.

And the grim air of danger that surrounds him.

"You put those on yourself," I say softly. "Not like the tigers."

"To me that's what the story is about. The things we do to ourselves. The way we hurt ourselves and mark ourselves."

It's a cautionary tale. He's warning me away from him.

I don't say anything until we reach the thin, sagging palm tree that marks the perimeter of the Tropicana motel. I feel a little sick imagining a tiny version of Kip, a little boy watching his mother mourn the life she wanted. I feel sick imagining the tattoo gun piercing an older Kip's skin while he looked on, thinking he deserved it as some kind of penance—as some kind of warning to the world around him.

But he has no idea what I deserve. "I'm sorry for

what happened to her. But I'm not her."

"I know that."

"And you can't save me or whatever you're trying to do here."

A sad smile flickers across his face. "I know that too. That isn't what I'm doing here."

He hands me my bag and stands with his arms at his sides as I start to walk away. My fists tighten on the straps of my bag. I stop, staring straight ahead, away from him.

After a beat, I ask, "Why are you here then?"

It can't just be for sex. He could get that in the Grand. Why does he want to spend time with me?

But when I look back, the sidewalk is empty. He's already gone.

CHAPTER TEN

I THINK ABOUT the feel of his hand around mine all day—warm, dry, and protective. It's the last feeling I need to be most worried about. *Protective.* Am I having some kind of breakdown? Am I losing touch with reality? Because Kip is a customer, the roughest kind. He's not my white knight. It's men like him I need saving from.

But not tonight, because he doesn't show up. Not even when I've danced my third song, not when I've worked the floor. A different man takes me to the back rooms, and I tell myself I'm not disappointed. I made the money I needed to, even if my hands smell like cheap cologne and come. I'm safe another day. That's all I can ask for. That's all I can want.

So I head back onto the floor and find a rumpled suit to feel me up. He does it discreetly, copping a feel while only paying for a lap dance on the public floor. I let him because it's easier than making a scene—and wince when he pinches instead of pets.

He grins, drunk and sideways. "Let me take you home, Honey."

My eyes flutter closed briefly. I'm tired of saying no. "I can't do that, but I can put on a show for you, right here."

His hand closes around my wrist—hard. "I want more than a show, you little tease."

I'm tired of saying no, but I'm even more tired of being ignored. "Let go of me," I say evenly.

Of course that just makes him squeeze tighter, until I wince. I know there'll be bruises tomorrow. I'll have to use my foundation around my wrist. All in a day's work.

Then someone is standing behind me. I feel their presence and a sense of relief. But it's a disappointment when he speaks.

"You heard the lady," he says. Not Kip.

The man looks up at Blue, clearly unaware of the threat he's under. He winks. "I heard, but I come here so I don't have to listen to them talk."

Blue does something fast and painful to the man's wrist, and then I'm free. I stand up and back away. It's one thing to mess with one of us, but messing with Blue is a really stupid move. Blue is a ticking time bomb. I don't want to be near him when he goes off.

"You're done," he tells the man. His voice is low, but everyone is watching now. They know what's happening—and they came here for a show, after all.

The man doesn't leave. "What the hell? I didn't touch her. She was just a whiny bitch."

"Then you won't mind not seeing her. I don't want to see your ugly face in the club again."

For a second it looks like the man will fight Blue, which would be insane because Blue is twice as big and three times as tough. The guy is a used-up frat boy, trying to find his kicks after a long day at the office. Whereas Blue is two hundred and fifty pounds of tatted muscle. But a few drinks and a bruised ego can make a person dumb.

The guy stands up, hands curled into fists. "Who the fuck do you—"

And maybe I am having a mental breakdown, because I reach for him then. I place a hand on the arm of this stranger. "Just go," I say softly. "It'll only be worse if you stay."

I'm nobody. Hasn't he just said as much? Not big and strong and intimidating like Blue. But the man seems to hear me. His eyes focus on mine for a second, and he takes a small step back. He mutters and curses under his breath as he grabs his jacket and walks away, but at least he doesn't start a fight.

When he is gone, Blue stares at me. He still looks pissed. If anything, he looks *more* pissed. "What the fuck?" he says.

My eyes widen. He's pissed at me? "I didn't start anything with him. I didn't complain."

He shakes his head. "That's the fucking point, Honey. You never complain. But you let him touch you. I saw it."

I didn't let him do anything. As if it's up to me. "If you want me to complain every time someone cops a feel, that's going to be all night long."

Something flickers in his eyes. Anger? Regret? Then

he snorts and looks away. "You're done too."

What? My heart skips a beat. I need this job. Travel is the most dangerous thing we can do. Two girls on the bus would mean attention. Someone to remember us when my father sent people asking. And I knew he would. He'd never give up. "I didn't do anything," I whispered.

I didn't complain. That should have been enough. It was what I'd been trained to do.

"For tonight," Blue said gruffly. "You're done for tonight. Can't dance like that anyway."

I don't know what he's talking about until I feel a drop trail down my cheek. Only then do I realize I've started crying. Which means my mascara is surely running. I must look awful. My throat tightens. "I'll come back tomorrow."

Blue just grunts.

I almost run off the floor, all too conscious of the eyes on me. There are always eyes on me. Everything is a performance. I don't even bother changing out of my sheer bra and panties. I just tug sweatpants and a tank top on and push out the door, my eyes hot with tears. But I can't go home like this. Not yet.

The more I feel exposed, the more I need to be alone.

So I make a turn around the building and grab the fire escape. Metal creaks as I haul myself the four feet off the ground and climb the rest of the way up. I dump the duffel bag without preamble and move into a plié. Grand plié. Over and over, fast enough to trip and fall, but I don't care. I want to fall.

"Honey," a low voice says.

And I do trip. I'm lucky I don't twist my ankle, but I manage to take the brunt of it on my palms. Then a strong pair of hands is helping me up, dusting the grime off my pants, inspecting my torn palms.

"Jesus," he says. "I didn't mean to scare you."

I look up at him, face shadowed in the moonlight. He's so beautiful.

And so cruel to make me want him.

I push away, ready to go back down the stairs, but I slide on the loose gravel that collects on the rooftop like snowdrifts. My body pitches forward, far enough over that I see the glistening street and let out a shriek. Then strong hands grasp my waist and pull me back—hard. I'm flush against a wall. Not made of brick, this wall. It's muscle and will, steady strength and heartbreak.

"Thank you," I say, my voice low and rough like the floor we're on.

I'm still breathing too hard, my heart beating too fast. I was so close to falling. And the scariest part is the relief I would have felt.

"You're always afraid, aren't you?" he murmurs against my ear.

I can't see his expression; I'm still facing away from him. His hands are still on my hips. But I can imagine his eyes when he says it, that mix of curiosity and reluctance. As if he's intrigued by me but he doesn't want to be.

I can feel him thinking instead. He's trying to figure me out. He's trying to burrow inside me until he sees how I work. But it will never work, because I'm not real. I'm smoke and mirrors—a magic trick. If he looks too closely, I'll disappear.

I pull away and face him.

He's a study in textures—the shadowed stubble on his jaw, the dark pools of his eyes. The worn leather of his jacket and the thick denim of his jeans. He is his own planet, terrain to be explored, mountains to climb and oceans to drown in. My fingers itch to touch him, though I'm not sure where I would start. I think his hair, because I want to know if he can be soft there, at least. Because the rest of him is so hard.

But I don't touch him. "What do you want?"

He looks away and blows out a breath. "To give you something."

"Something else?" I still have the Taser he gave me in my bag. Not that I could have used it on him. He caught me totally by surprise just now.

He reaches into his jacket and pulls something out. This time I don't need to hold it to know what it is. I don't extend my hand either.

Instead a strangled sound escapes me. "A gun?"

His expression is almost bashful, a sharp contrast to the sleek heavy metal thing he holds so expertly. "I was thinking...the Taser isn't enough. Not in this neighborhood. Not with you working here."

"Is that even legal?" I squeak.

His low laugh is my answer. "Do you want to put your name in a database?"

"No, but I don't want a gun either." I'm more likely to accidentally shoot somebody than protect myself with that. The Taser was already a big step for me. The gun is downright terrifying. It's too much. I can't take it.

He seems to understand that. He nods and puts it back in his jacket. "If you change your mind..."

I stare at him, both confused and captivated. What strange gifts he's brought for me. First the Taser. Now the gun. They're both so violent. I hate violence. But they are also protection—and I need protection.

He's like a cat bringing me a dead mouse as a gift. Disturbing. And sweet.

"Do you want me to go?" he asks.

I should tell him yes. I should tell him to leave. "Don't go."

Christ, I'm in too deep. How long has it been since I was attracted to a man? I'm not sure I ever have been. I had a crush on the bodyguard, but that was girlish—despite the adult things he did to me. There had barely been time, or opportunity, to look at men before I got engaged to Byron. And now I'm so far into this man, into Kip, that I don't know how to back away.

Kip smiles a little. "Then I'll stay."

I narrow my eyes, playfully suspicious. "Now that you have me here, what are you going to do with me?"

His smile gives me all kinds of suggestions. "That depends."

"On what?"

"On what you like."

Oh, he's good. A little spark of pleasure lights up in me. It may just be a line he gives all the girls, but it works. It's more seductive than his scruff or his muscles or his boots—the idea that he cares. I dance every day, trying to please men I don't even know. And here is this one, trying to please me.

"I like to dance."

"I'd like to see that."

"Then why don't you come into the club?"

"Not like that. I'd like to see you dance the way you want to."

I'm not sure that's even possible. If I know he's there, I'll be dancing for him. I've been trained too well—by Byron, by my father. I even perform for Clara, in a way. There is no freedom with other people. Only in being alone.

"No dancing," I say, strangely disappointed.

"Then let's lie down," he says gently. Maybe he knows how hard this is for me, to get close. Maybe it's hard for him too. "We can look at the stars and let them dance for us."

My heart clenches with something like wistfulness.

He's not even gone, but I already miss him. I've had so little kindness lately. Or ever. And here he is with a whole weapons cache full of kindness. *The killing game.* I remember what Blue said about him. Even Ivan warned me away.

Kip stands there looking gruff and intimidating, like he would take on the whole world for looking at him sideways. There are scars on his knuckles that say he tried. And there's a bend in his nose that says he's lost. But despite all that violence, he touches me with desire.

He already has my body, already bought and used up. But he wants something else.

He wants me.

✧   ✧   ✧

MY FATHER LOVED my mother. I was young when she died—when he killed her—but I remember that much.

I remember how he doted on her, giving her everything she asked for and more. I remember how she would laugh and tell him not to spoil her. I would sneak out of my bed when they threw parties. Even in a crowd of people, all dressed in elaborate gowns and tuxedos, they were easy to spot. She always had a smile, and he only had eyes for her. They would dance in the middle of the room, eclipsing all the other people.

And then one day my father came to me, eyes red and swollen from crying, voice thick with grief, to tell me she had died. I think I knew then he had done it. It was the lack of revenge that told me. If anyone else had shot her, he would have destroyed the whole city to avenge her instead of holding a small closed-casket funeral in the rain. A casket I wanted to believe was empty. But was it really better to believe she had abandoned me?

Maybe that was why I slept with my bodyguard. It

had been a way to be close to my mother, to be like her, years after she was gone. Of course then I didn't understand that a twenty-one-year-old man interested in a fourteen-year-old girl was wrong. I don't think he even cared about my body. He was a rush junkie, and I was his fix. Fucking the boss's daughter was just another risk. The men on my father's payroll didn't exactly have printed resumes and pension plans.

They never lived long enough to need one.

On the roof of the strip club, we are a thousand miles away from that world. Far away from tuxedos and ball gowns. Far from love and jealousy and revenge.

There is only a man who wants to fuck me. And touch me and make me hump his boot.

A man who will pay for the right.

Inside the walls of the club, he pays in cash. On the roof he pays with gifted weapons and an unexpected gentleness. He pays with thoughtfulness, but it's a currency all the same. And so I let myself relax. He puts aside the gun and lays his jacket down like a blanket. Then I'm lying with my head on his arm, looking up.

"How long have you lived here?" I ask.

I don't mean for the question to come out, but it does. We shouldn't get personal. Fucking and sucking, but no questions. And no answers.

"Not long," he says, looking up at the sky. "I don't stay put very long."

"That sounds nice," I murmur. Never putting down roots. Never having them yanked out.

"Sometimes. Other times I wonder what it would be like to have everything I need, right at my fingertips. Food, a bed. Sex."

"You have those things." It's not supposed to be suggestive. I just mean he can buy them, in a restaurant or a motel. Or a strip club.

But when he looks at me, there's heat in his eyes. And resolve, as if he's finally taking what's his. The words change and tighten. They become about the taste of him and the warm jacket we lie on. They become about the sex I'll soon give him.

His gaze sweeps over my body, stretched out. I'm wearing yoga pants and a tank top, but the way he looks at me, I'm already naked. He strips me with just his eyes, leaving me bare and vulnerable and strangely unashamed.

"You're beautiful," he says, his voice hoarse.

I flinch, because it's what Byron used to tell me. Of course when he said it, it was a compliment to himself, praise for finding the perfect accessory to his life.

Kip notices. "You don't like that word."

"No. Yes. I don't know." I laugh softly. "It's complicated. I look like my mother."

That's what my father always told me, with the bitter light of grief in his eyes.

There must be grief in my eyes too, because Kip says, "She's gone."

"It was a long time ago. I thought I was over it, but for some reason I think of her a lot more now." Maybe because Clara is paying for her sins. Maybe because I am too.

He is quiet a moment. "I think we never really get over the past. It's always shaping us."

Then how is it shaping you? But I am careful not to ask that question. I think with the quietude and the starlit intimacy, he might actually tell me. And then where would I be? I can't care about a man. I can't care about anything but my sister. All I can carve out for myself is a single night with a man I choose.

Because it isn't really about payment when I take his hand and place it on my breast.

A breath leaves him on a sigh as his hand cups me. Broad fingers stroke my skin above the edge of my tank top. A heavy palm warms me through the fabric. I can still hear him saying I'm beautiful, but he holds back now, thoughtful. "I see you," he finally murmurs. "Only you."

It's his way of grounding me in the present, and it's working. He does see me, because he doesn't know anything of my past. He doesn't know where I came from or where I'm going. I'm so tired of being my father's daughter, my mother's daughter, my sister's protector. For this moment I'm just me. I'm only a warm body for him to use, and I need to be that for him.

"Do you want me to dance for you now?" I whisper even though I said I wouldn't.

He shakes his head slowly, eyes dark and solemn. "You don't have to dance. You don't even have to move. Just let me make you feel good."

I don't remember what good is anymore, but his strong hands show me. They push up the hem of my tank top, exposing me to the cool night air. They trace circles over my skin. He pulls the fabric over my breasts, sucking in a breath when he sees the lace bra I have on.

His hand looks dark against the bright red, powerful over the sheer fabric. He strokes his thumb back and forth across the tip of my breast, hardening the nipple until it makes a point. My body responds to him without me doing anything—like he said, I don't even have to move. My hands remain at my sides, my head resting on the folded edge of the jacket that is my pillow. My head is propped enough that I can watch him stroke my breasts while I lay passive, and it's so easy to lie there, so easy to let him, so easy to feel pleasure arc through me without moving a muscle.

He runs a finger over the curves of my small breasts, traces the lines of the bra. Then he slips his hand underneath, touching me without seeing. It is a shocking warmth, his hand on my breast. These breasts I've bared to so many men. They are covered now—by him.

The lacy fabric stretches over his hand, pushed up with no room to give. Underneath, his hand shifts, finding my nipple between thumb and forefinger. He squeezes gently, and a soft sound escapes me, like a whimper.

"You feel so good. You feel like fucking heaven." He rolls my nipple between his fingers. "This is what I dream about. Keeping you in bed, bringing you food and wine, touching you as much as I want."

My eyes fall shut, imagining his fantasy. Instead of a stripper in a seedy club, I am his personal sex slave, wrapped in silks and desire. My body grows warm at the thought, wet at the core. "Kip."

"Would you like that?" he murmurs. I think he knows exactly what he's doing to me. "Would you lie there and let me touch you as long as I want to? Even when you fall asleep, I'd keep my hands on you. On these pretty breasts. On your pussy."

And then, as if to illustrate his point, he removes his hand from my bra and slides it down, underneath the waistband of my pants. He doesn't stop until he dips his fingers into the slickness pooling there.

"Fuck, you do like this." He actually sounds shocked.

It makes me laugh—though it's almost a giggle. I didn't know I was even capable of making that sound, but then a lot of things are a surprise tonight. Apparently I'm the type of girl who can drink alcohol with a boy she likes, who will let him finger her while she plays the docile, innocent victim.

Of course, I'm not innocent. And I'm not really sure I like him.

"Don't stop," I say.

That earns me a slight smile. "I wasn't planning to."

He runs his fingers through the wetness there, but without purpose, without the speed I'd need to get off. He's just feeling me, exploring me, the same way he did my breasts. My legs are already parted enough to give him access, but without planning it, my knees fall apart. It's an invitation, and he doesn't miss a beat, pushing deeper. But still with lazy strokes.

Not enough. A whimper escapes me.

And it sounds like acceptance. It must be acceptance, because he pushes up and slings a leg over my chest. He pulls off his shirt, and I can see his chest in full glory, broad and strong, covered in tribal tattoos and scars. He's dangerous. He's primal.

For tonight he's mine.

Then he's undoing his jeans, pulling out his cock. He presses the tip to my lips—without foreplay or finesse. His body blocks the moonlight. The only thing I can see is the shadow of him. The only thing I can smell is the musk of his precum.

He paints my lips with the salty liquid, the same way he used my wetness to dampen my nipples. But this time he isn't the one cleaning it off. This time it's me licking my lips, tasting him for the first time.

He tastes like danger and pleasure, like risk and reward.

"Open for me," he groans.

I open my lips, letting him inside, almost grateful, relishing the way his whole body stiffens. I breathe him in, the salty scent of his cock, already smelling of me and him—as if we've had sex. He stares down at me as I swirl my tongue around the head of his cock, and I don't look away.

There are rules, about looking him in the eye. About

using a condom, even for this.

But I'm breaking them. My tongue and my lips and even the edge of my teeth work to give him pleasure, pushing faster and harder than I've ever done before—not because I want it to end, but because I know it will. And when this is over, I want him to remember me.

Foolish. Reckless. I don't care. Right now I want that as much as survival—more.

He grunts and finds a rhythm, and I match my sucking to him, opening my throat to let him in deeper, using my sucks and my tongue in tandem to push him over the edge. Just like he pushed me. It's a double-edged sword between us, but right now he's the one being cut. He's the one shuddering, groaning, almost humping the floor as he fucks my mouth.

A lock of my hair falls into my face, jerked by the rough motion of his body and mine. He reaches down…and carefully smooths the lock from my forehead. Even though I'm lying on a leather jacket, arms pinned by my sides, getting fucked, being used—the touch is almost tender.

"Christ," he gasps, and then warm come fills my mouth.

I swallow it quickly, only to find more spurting from the tip. He has so much come, as if he hasn't climaxed in forever, like he's been saving it all for me. I swallow again and again, until only the faint salty flavor of him remains, and he pulls away.

He runs his thumb down my cheek, then lower,

wiping away a drop of his come from the corner of my lips. "Thank you," he says.

I let him tuck the blanket around me, warming me up. Only then do I realize I'm cold. Freezing. I'm still shivering, until he slips under with me, wrapping his strong arms around me. "Shh," he soothes.

"I didn't say anything," I say.

I feel his smile. "I heard you anyway, Honey. I always do. You don't even have to say anything. You just have to feel, and I can hear it like a goddamn church bell."

"And you're a religious man?" I ask, smiling sleepily.

"No, never. But you make me want to be. I want to worship you."

His cock is already half-erect against my leg. He follows through on his promise, worshipping me with his lips and tongue and fingers until I writhe on that roof, until I open my mouth and choke out incoherent words, plead'ng, crying, needing, while the heavy moon looks on with satisfaction.

His cock spreads me wide, filling me until I can only rock my hips up, riding the edge.

He grunts on every thrust, a primal sound that spurs me on. His breath is hot against my skin. His hips spreading my legs wide. I'm completely invaded by him, taken over, wanting more.

"Please, please, please," I beg, shameless, free of the shackles I wear below this roof, onstage.

But it's too much. I'm too loud. Especially when he moves to hit a different spot inside me. I moan, and his hand comes up to cover my mouth. That is what pushes me over—the rough feel of his palm on my lips, being quieted by him, controlled. I come in a burst of color and sound, sensation rolling over me, making me clench around his cock as it pulses with come.

CHAPTER ELEVEN

IT'S CLOSE TO dawn when I climb down the fire escape, careful not to rattle the metal too much. I'll have to hurry to make it back to Clara in time. That's the excuse I have for leaving without waking him up. Okay, I'm not just leaving. I'm sneaking away. But Kip is asleep. I must have drifted off at some point too.

It will be easier for both of us if I'm gone when he wakes up. We aren't going to run away together. This isn't a fairy tale. I won't make the same mistakes my mother did. I know better than to trust a man.

I know better than to love one.

Candy is leaning against the brick wall. She takes the cigarette from her lips and blows smoke in my direction. She looks me up and down, clearly unimpressed by what she sees. "Didn't we tell you not to get involved with the customers?"

Of course they did—and the worst part is, they're right. There's no way this ends well for me. "I'm not involved," I lie.

She laughs, low and bitter. "Doesn't get more involved than fucking outside the club. Let me guess, he didn't have to pay you for that one. That was just for fun."

I flinch because I hadn't even thought to ask for payment. What we did suddenly feels cheap. And that's what it is...cheap. "Stop," I whisper.

"Is that what you told him?" Her voice is taunting, her eyes whip-sharp. I've never seen her like this. I can only think I've earned her wrath for ignoring her advice. For keeping my secrets.

"We just talked."

A roll of her pretty eyes. "I heard you up there."

My face burns with embarrassment. I climaxed up there, not nearly quiet enough. I *enjoyed* myself up there, and maybe that's the most embarrassing of all. I finally figured out how amazing sex could be, and it was on the roof of a strip club.

I hear the metal clang, and then Kip is working his way down. He's got his shirt back on and his jeans and his boots, and damn does he look good in them.

Then I glance at Candy and realize she caught me checking him out. I blush, even though I think it's bullshit. The men can ogle us all night long, but I'm not supposed to appreciate a fine masculine body?

He nods at Candy, his voice rough from sleep. "Morning."

She snorts. "Get yourself a free fuck, did you?"

"That's not how I would've put it, no," he says, though he doesn't seem surprised by her sharp words.

"I bet."

"You have a problem with me?"

"Several, actually." She smirks. "I know who you are."

Her words sink in like ice through my skin. She knows something about Kip that I don't. Unless she's lying. But his expression goes completely blank, stripped of emotion. And I know it's real.

"Good for you," he says, just as flat.

Her gaze slides over to me, her eyes way too innocent to be real. "Does she know you're *related?*"

"What are you talking about?" I ask. *Related to who?*

"Why don't you fill her in?" she tells Kip. Then she drops her cigarette and strolls back into the club, using her stage walk to swing her hips.

I turn to Kip. "Tell me."

He shakes his head. His eyes are opaque, as solid as the brick wall behind me. "There's nothing to tell. My brother is an asshole. He had a reputation around here."

"So do you, apparently."

That makes him smile. But I know that's not the whole story. He's definitely hiding something. Candy knows he's related to *some asshole,* but why would she think I'd care about that? It brings home the fact that there's a lot I don't know about Kip. More than just who his brother is. I don't even know his last name.

The he does something that makes my gut clench. He reaches to his back pocket—for the gun? Maybe he'll try to give it to me again. But I can't take it. Or his wallet? For money. And not just because of Candy's jab. He once told me he'd always pay for the privilege. He promised me that. It had been his line in the sand, but I'm erasing it.

I know it's messier this way.

"No," I say. "Don't."

He cocks his head to the side. "Don't what?"

"Don't make this cheap."

EVERYTHING IS HAZY and dark. Not like the stage, too bright to see. Blinding me. The woods are so dark. I can just barely make out the pale path ahead of me. I follow it, hoping to find an open space soon. Somewhere safe to rest. But the trees seem to grow closer and closer on either side until I can barely breathe. In the dark wall of the jungle I can see green eyes blink at me. I can hear the hiss of a snake.

I bolt awake.

I'm drenched in sweat. Like in my dream, it's dark. I can barely make out the faded floral bedspread covering me. The walls are pitch-black and looming. But this isn't a jungle. It's the motel room.

My heart is pounding a million times a minute. I pull myself out of bed and get a drink of water from the bathroom. Then I stand beside Clara's bed and watch her sleep.

I get comfortable watching, sitting on the edge, tucking a foot under me. Even with my eyes adjusted to the dark, I can't make out her face. It doesn't matter. I know her face as well as my own. I can see the bedspread rise and fall ever so slightly. That's what matters. Maybe it's creepy to watch her sleep. I don't care. As long as she's breathing, as long as she's safe, then what I'm doing is worth something. I'm worth something.

She must sense me there, because she stirs. She rolls over, toward me. Does she have bad dreams too?

Her eyes blink open. They're bright in the darkness. Not green, though. Not scary.

"Honor," she says, voice thick with sleep.

"Go back to sleep," I say, soothing. "Everything's fine."

I hope I haven't scared her. And I haven't. She trusts me to protect her. The only problem is I don't know how. My life has never been about safety. It's a foreign idea, like landing on the moon. Or falling in love. All I know is how to survive.

"Are you okay?" she asks, still in that distant voice. She must have one foot still in her dreams.

"I'm fine," I promise. And I know I should leave it at that, but something pushes me onward. She's vulnerable now. She's more honest than she'd ever be waking. "Are you okay, Clara? Are you happy here?"

"Not happy. Can't be happy."

I flinch. I should have known the answer—maybe I did know all along—but I wasn't prepared to hear it. Not in the middle of the night, so soon after the nightmare.

"God, Clara," I whisper. "What have I done?"

I know we couldn't have stayed there. I could never

let Byron or his friends touch her. But this isn't okay either, this shitty motel room. *Can't be happy.*

"She's hurt," Clara whispers. "She's hurting."

Who is she talking about? Herself? I search for my voice, for some comfort I can give. "No one's going to hurt you, baby."

"They'll kill him."

I shiver.

Her hand reaches over the blanket and grasps mine. She feels ice-cold. I squeeze her hand. In those final moments she'd been fully lucid. I could feel her slipping away now, back into sleep. That is for the best. She probably won't even remember this tomorrow.

They'll kill him.

The truth is, they probably already did kill him. A young man who lived on our father's estate, the son of one of his guards, helped us escape. I wait until her breathing evens out and her grip around my hand loosens before I get up. I'm still nowhere close to sleep, so I wander over to the window. The drapes in the motel room are heavy and wide. They block out most of the light. So when I push them aside to peek through, even the faint light pricks my eyes.

The sidewalk is empty. Everything is still and quiet.

My hand brushes the Madonna statue, and it wobbles on the sill. It's light, hollow. Made of plastic. I'm not sure who would buy a statue like this as a religious symbol. It's too irreverent. But we're using it as one.

She looks over us, this mother holding her child. She

protects us. It's worked so far.

I put my fingertip on the top of her head. *Just a little while longer. Once I get proof against my father, I can use it as leverage. We'll be free of him then.*

We won't need the protection of a burned-out light-up Madonna anymore.

✧   ✧   ✧

MY FATHER IS a descendent from one of the original leading families in Las Vegas. Due to the path of our family tree and criminal politics, he didn't play a major role in the larger organization. But he was still respected. Still feared.

He would tell me bedtime stories with *delitto d'onore.* Honor killings. About men who disrespected their families and had to be put down. I didn't realize until later that *delitto d'onore* is why he might have killed my mother. Didn't realize it until later that it's why he might kill me...if he finds me.

Maybe one day I'd figure out what honor really meant, because I couldn't be like him. I couldn't give Clara away to one of Byron's friends. I couldn't let her be all but sold to a monster—all in the name of family honor.

Like I had been.

I'm done with honor. I'm ready to be bad. To break the rules for more than just money. Except, of course, the man that I want to break them with doesn't come back. For five nights. Five long nights of dancing in a smoky room, of evading grabbing hands. The girls figure out something is up with me.

"I told you not to date them," Lola says.

I don't look up as I pull sweatpants and a tank top on. I'm naked underneath, but the soft fleece is a relief after the harsh elastic and even harsher lights onstage. "Who says I did?"

"You have the look. Let me guess. He bought you dinner, got a blowjob, then didn't call again."

That's close enough to the truth that I can't refute it. But it's not the whole truth. It doesn't take into account that he seems to want more than sex. It doesn't take into account that I can't give him that.

"It doesn't matter," I say. "It's over."

Lola rolls her eyes. "Of course it's over. We're not the girls they take home to mama. We're not the ones they keep."

I shudder. I'd been the girl that got kept before. If I was lucky, I'd never have to go back. "Maybe I'm the one who didn't call him. It's not only men who want sex with no strings attached."

She laughs. "Oh, sweetie, you've got so many strings you'll never get free."

My heart clenches because she's right. I'm running and running, trying to stay safe, desperate to keep Clara safe, but I'm failing. It's easy to see that I'm failing, standing in the dressing room of the strip club, feeling pathetic over some guy. Over a customer, of all people. I'm working as hard as I can, giving up everything—even my dignity—and it isn't enough.

You'll never get free.

A knot forms in my throat. I couldn't speak even if I knew what to say.

Lola's face falls. "Shit. I didn't—"

"Don't worry about it," I say, my voice rough. And I push past her before she can stop me.

CHAPTER TWELVE

I ENTER THE dressing room the next day and immediately know I'm in huge trouble. The room is empty. No Candy, no Lola, no other girls. Just Ivan, sitting on my stool.

He's waiting for me.

I can see that from the stillness of his body, the watchfulness despite his casual pose. He looks huge on that stool where I sit, huge next to the vanity I use. It's a reminder of how much power he has—both physically and otherwise—and I'm guessing he planned for that.

"Honor."

I flinch, and I'm not even sure why. No one else is here, but it hurts to hear him say my real name. I'm not really Honey—that's just a facade. But I'm not Honor either, that locked-up girl back home. I'm someone else, someone without a name. "Is something wrong?"

"Apparently." He pauses, watching me. Like he wants me to confess.

"Did you find something about my mother?"

"I'm not sure why I'd be expected to hold up my agreement when you aren't holding up yours."

Fear grips my chest. "I'm dancing for you. That was

our agreement."

"And as one of my dancers, you do what I tell you. So if I tell you to stay away from Kip, you stay away."

I flinch. "How did you—"

"Does it matter? I find out about everything that happens in this club eventually. And you've been spending too much time with him for it to go unnoticed. Private dances are one thing. But outside the club? You deliberately disobeyed me."

I bite my lip against all the apologies and pleas that want to slip out. I've lived my life under a powerful man's thumb. I know what it is to beg and scrabble for the smallest freedom. But I left to get away from that. It's a hard thing, being used by every man I meet, placating their demands to earn a little more time. Sometimes I feel like I'm buying freedom with freedom, debt piling on debt, until I'll owe the whole world just to die.

But he has something I want. Something I need. Information.

I can see the gleam in his eyes. He wouldn't have come to a bargaining table without the upper hand.

"I'm sorry," I finally say, although too late and insincere to be useful.

His eyes darken. He stands up and approaches me. I shrink back from the dark look in his eyes. He doesn't stop until I'm backed up against the wall.

"Did he fuck you that well?" he whispers, mouth an inch from my cheek. "You couldn't say no?"

He's just trying to scare me. I know that. I can recognize that fact, but it doesn't stop it from working.

"All this time he never comes into my club. Now suddenly he's a regular customer." Ivan runs a finger down my cheek. "Although I guess we can't really call him a customer."

"I just…" My voice wavers. "I didn't think it would hurt anyone."

"So worried about other people. When really it's you that'll end up hurt."

"No, he wouldn't—"

"Maybe you should get down on your knees again. I can see what you've been giving him."

My heart pounds. I offered him this in his office, but it's different out here in the dressing room. And maybe it's different because of Kip too. He's changing me. He's making me stronger, and in my life that's not really a good thing.

"No," I whisper.

"What did you say?"

"She said no." The voice comes from the doorway. Both Ivan and I look over. *Kip.*

Oh Jesus. He's never come to the dressing room. Why is he here now?

That's answered for me when I get a glimpse of Candy behind him. She must have known Ivan was going to talk to me, must have known I was in trouble. And she called Kip to protect me. But it will only make it worse. Ivan and I are tinder, brittle and dry. Kip is the match.

He looks seriously pissed, brows furrowed and

mouth set in a grim line. "Honey."

Just that one word and somehow I'm going to him, obeying his tacit command, choosing him over Ivan before I can process what a monumentally awful idea that is. Kip is just a customer. *Not even that.* But Ivan is my boss. He's also a man holding the key to my past. I need him to like me. I need to be on my knees in front of him right now, but instead I'm behind Kip as he steps in front of me—protecting me with his body.

Ivan raises an eyebrow at Kip. "Sticking your nose in my business?"

Kip is like some kind of avenging angel, standing in front of me, fearless. "She said no."

Ivan laughs, incredulous. "She's one of my girls. She does what I say, when I say. If I want her to fuck half of Tanglewood, she'll spread her fucking legs."

Kip doesn't immediately react, but I feel his anger spread like wildfire, forming around the three of us, locking us in this battle. When he speaks, it is quiet, barely above the roar in my ears. "She belongs to me now."

The words ring through me like a bell, echoing inside me. What? Ivan sounds surprised too. "She's a stripper."

"Not anymore."

I can't catch my breath. What the hell is he talking about? *She belongs to me now.* It's barbaric. And considering I need Ivan, a really inconvenient time to be getting possessive. So why does pleasure spread from the inside out, warming me, raising goose bumps on my skin?

Then I can't hold it in anymore—I peek around Kip's arm to see Ivan looking calculating. I expect him to say something sharp or threatening. His power around here is well known. The men who come to visit him are scary characters in their own right, but they are always deferential to Ivan. If this were a high school yearbook, he'd get voted *most likely to terrify*, and I'm terrified for Kip.

But then something strange happens.

Ivan's gaze turns considering. He sizes Kip up. His gaze flicks to me. Acknowledgement turns his eyes cool. "Yours?"

"You have something to say to her, go through me."

And just like that, he backs down. Ivan's gaze flicks to me, then back to Kip. "You can tell your girlfriend that what she's looking for isn't here. It never was."

My mother. He means she never arrived in Tanglewood. It's hard to breathe. I always knew she never left Las Vegas, but hearing it confirmed still hurts. I guess when you see that gleaming closed casket, there's always a part of you that hopes. Some small part of me that imagined her finding some other way, driving off into the sunset. Alive. Safe. Betrayed by both her husband and lover.

Ivan strides from the room, leaving us alone.

I swallow hard. Kip may have won this round over Ivan, but I can't trust that. And no wonder, considering what happened to my mother. I have issues. But I can't leave Kip either. Can't do anything but stand beside him. He defended me from Ivan. He's protected me all along.

And now he's claimed me.

✧　✧　✧

THERE'S A MOTORCYCLE waiting a few yards away. Kip walks over and picks up the helmet.

He holds it out. "Let's go."

It doesn't even occur to me to walk away. He came for me; I'm going with him. I can't offer him any kind of relationship or commitment. At some point I'll have to explain that, but not now—not so soon after he stalked into the Grand and shielded me with his own body. Not right after he said I was his. He's won this. He's earned me. It's a fantasy we can live together for one night, an hourglass with each kernel of sand bringing my enemies closer to me, one more breath facing the open mouth of a gun.

"Where?" I ask, already taking the helmet anyway, because it doesn't matter where we go. *Anywhere.* "I need to be back by sunrise."

The corner of his lips lifts, and I'm riveted by the scruff that frames them. The whiskers that are sharp against my skin, leaving red marks. The mouth so soft and talented. "Already planning to get rid of me?"

The truth is we were always bound to end. The truth is we should never have started. "I want every second I can get with you," I tell him honestly. To prove my point, I put the helmet on.

Take me away.

And though I can't voice my desire, he seems to know. He grabs my hand and steadies me as I hook my leg over the bike. It's bigger than I expected—taller and wider. I've never been on a motorcycle before. I was more likely to ride in the back of my father's Rolls. At least when I was allowed to leave the house. My feet come off the ground. Between the helmet and his broad back, I can't see anything. I'm completely at his mercy like this.

"Hold on." The words are more a rumble through his body—and into mine—than a sound.

I wrap my arms around his waist, soaking up his solidity like a cat in the sun. It's been missing from my life, only coming in my dreams: safety. Stability. I take it all into my body, store it deep, hoarding the feeling for the time when I'm on the run again.

He's wrong for me. Dangerous.

Desire doesn't ask questions. Neither does love.

The roar of the engine is deafening—almost blinding, like the lights onstage. There's a moment. There's a shiver down my spine. There's a doorway into a new place. But this isn't a stage. These aren't hands to grope me. This place is the rush of air over my skin as we take off. It's the steady rumble of the machine beneath my legs, the hard body of the man I'm holding.

I don't know how long we ride, but I never want it to end. When it stops, the clock will start ticking again. Ticking down the time I have with him, another grain of sand dropped. But while we're on the bike, racing down a street I don't even recognize, headed nowhere and everywhere, I feel the freedom I've been searching for.

I look to the side, but the buildings are gone. In their place are streaks of rust and gray. Brushstrokes in every drab color, made mysterious by night. This is the way he sees the world every day, I realize. As art.

The painting turns to green and brown, and I know we've left the city.

Anxiety shivers through me. What if he's taking me out here for some darker purpose? What if he doesn't bring me back? I almost laugh, though it's a macabre amusement. What if I've escaped one monster only to find another?

But then I realize Clara will run if I don't come back. She promised.

She'll be safe. Alive. Not like my mother.

Not like me.

And I let my worries go. I paint them on the canvas we make, like bread crumbs I could use to find my way home.

Chapter Thirteen

THE SKY HAS turned a muted blue by the time we
arrive. I look around. There are only trees and grass
and a winding road that led us here. I don't know why
he's brought me to this place. There is a reason, though.
I read the secret in the tension of his body. He's got a
little half smile too, the kind that hides a surprise. It
makes my heart thump a little too hard, that smile—sexy
and impossibly sweet.

"Where are we?" I ask, musing. I don't think he'll tell
me.

And he doesn't. "Nowhere that's on a map."

He's really too pleased with himself. I think of Peter
Pan flying off into Neverland, taking Wendy with him. I
think of sword fights and fairies. That's how it feels in
the clearing—like magic.

Only magic isn't real. Flying isn't real either, even if
it felt like that on the back of his bike.

"You know, if I were another girl, I might be worried
about all this secrecy. You might have dug a ditch out
here for all I know."

His smile slips away, and I regret my words. Why
can't I just accept this moment for what it is? Why can't

I trust anyone? My insides churn, faster and harder. How did I get so broken?

His hand takes mine, warm and dry and comforting. "If that's what you think, why did you come with me?"

His words are soft, more curious than accusing.

"I'm not some other girl," I tell him. I've looked death in the face my whole life. My father is a murderer. My fiancé is a monster. "I'm afraid of dying, but I'm more afraid of never living."

Understanding flickers in his eyes. He knows I mean more than just drawing breath. More than just running. I dream of the day I can be safe enough to really enjoy life. To do more than survive.

It's why I came with him. He's a breath of life.

"It's nothing scary," he assures me. "It's…like a present."

My heart skips. "A present? Because your presents have a tendency to be scary."

That makes him laugh. "Not this one."

"What is it?" I tease him. "A battle ax? A sword?"

He just smiles mysteriously and leads me into the grass.

There is no path here. We follow the tree line, walking through lush grass already damp with dew. Then the trees break, revealing a structure standing at the top of a hill. Is it a house? But no, it is made entirely of windows. Or at least, there used to be windows. Now there are tall empty spaces where glass would go. It could almost pass for an old greenhouse except for the elaborate dome on the top.

And the turrets.

It reminds me of a woman. An old stately woman with gray hair and a serenity that only comes from experience. I don't look at her and think, *she once was beautiful.* I think, *she is beautiful.* Every wrinkle in her skin, every crack in the stone, stands for a secret she kept.

"What is this place?" I breathe.

He is quiet a moment. I look over to find him studying me, an uncertain light in his eyes. *He's studying me,* I realize, and that both unnerves and charms me, that he would be that interested in me, that he wants to see beneath the smooth, waxed surface of my skin.

"I'm not sure. The house is two klicks south of here. Or what's left of it. This was... a detached ballroom? An observatory? Maybe both."

A ballroom. That sounds right.

I'm too excited now. I let go of his hand and run ahead, finding the door even though every window is open. There is no actual door either, just an empty frame. I step inside and look up. The ceiling is faded, scrubbed from the inside each time a storm rages. But I can still see the painting of cherubic angels.

I can't even begin to guess when this place was built or how long it has lain abandoned, but somehow, a few panes of window have survived, mostly near the ceiling or the base, where they were partially protected by a turret outside. I couldn't see them from outside because they were too murky, too muted to reflect the moonlight. The gloom of them matched the gloom inside, camouflaged.

But here, I can see the windows clearly, blocking the sight of the trees. From inside I can see everything.

He is standing by the door when I look back. His arms are folded. He leans against the empty doorframe, his face shrouded in shadow. Somehow I'm in the middle of the room. I forgot myself for a moment, forgot to be worried. Forgot to be afraid.

I approach him slowly, feeling somehow shy. He's done filthy things to my body, and I've done them to him. But now I am just a girl who's been given a present by a boy.

I look down for a moment at my shoes and the marble floor beneath, made murky with time. "Not that I don't appreciate you bringing me here. But why?"

Of all the things he could have given me. He could have taken me to see a movie. He could have brought me a flower. Instead he took me here, knowing this would mean more than anything.

Not just why. How?

He doesn't move. Doesn't touch me. Doesn't take payment from my body, not yet. "I thought you might want to dance here." He nods toward the floor. "Like the roof."

Oh, but this isn't like the roof. It isn't uneven, with rusted metal bars jutting up from the concrete. It isn't covered in tiny pebbles, pieces of the structure itself crumbling away under the elements. Instead there is smooth marble—almost unbreakable, this floor. The wind has swept away any leaves. The rain has washed away any dirt. It almost gleams. Not like the roof at all.

I can't see him clearly. It is still too dark for that, but I can almost swear he's blushing. I'm surprised he even knows how to. It's not even a color, it's a feeling. Maybe it can only ever be something to feel, his generosity. His quiet acceptance of who and what I am.

My chest is too full, and my eyes are too wet. I consider dropping to my knees to thank him. I could make it so good.

Instead I reach up on my tiptoes and kiss his cheek. The growth of whiskers is scratchy against my lips, his skin warm under that.

"Thank you."

Then I leave him by the door, to watch me and wait as I dance like I'm alone. I start off slowly, plié, grand plié. And this time when I stretch my body in a grand *arabesque*, I am not wringing myself clean of unwanted hands—I am reaching. For him. For the sky beyond the painted ceiling and through the open window frames. I am reaching for a time and a place when I won't have to hide anymore.

My skin is slick with sweat by the time I have finished. Even then I don't want to be finished, but the tops of the trees are pink with pre-dawn light. I should go back.

I don't want to.

He meets me in the middle of the ballroom.

"I have time for one more dance," I tell him, suggestive.

"I can't dance."

That makes me laugh. "That isn't what I meant."

He doesn't smile. His face is more severe than ever—a rejection. "I know what you meant."

I frown, confused. "Kip?"

His face is like a stone wall. I wait for the branches to rise up, guarding their fortress. I wait for the sting of the thorns. He wants to hate me. He doesn't want to get close.

This time the brambles don't come.

This time he bends his head. I am too shocked to tilt my head. Too surprised to kiss him back. I stand there, passive, letting his lips press against mine, feeling his tongue slide along my lower lip. I have enough frame of mind to open, and he groans softly, taking the invitation and demanding more.

His hands curve around my hips, cupping my ass. I'm sweaty, but he doesn't seem to mind. No, he presses me flush against him, taking each of my panting breaths into his mouth, sipping the salt from my skin.

I rub my body against him, feeling his erection thick and stone hard in his jeans. I rock my hips against it, promising relief.

All at once he releases me. He turns away. I stare at the tall, broad line of his shoulders—moving up and down with his heavy, aroused breathing.

What the hell? Why did he stop?

Hesitantly I place a hand on his arm. He pulls away.

Dread fills me. "What did I do wrong?"

"Nothing," he says. But I can hear the lie in his voice.

"Kip?" I hate how timid I sound, how afraid. I never let my father or Byron see me like this. With them I always put up a strong front. They might hurt me and humiliate me, but they would never see me cry. But with Kip it feels inevitable. He tears down my bravery, leaving only hope.

"I'm not who you think I am."

❖ ❖ ❖

NO. I WANT to rewind the past five seconds and pretend he never said that.

"I'm not just a customer," he says, and I wish that were a lie. Maybe a random guy at a strip club isn't good relationship material to other women. But to me he's everything I could want. I hadn't worked out how we might be together beyond this night or the next. But I'd hoped.

And now he's telling me something serious, something dark, his voice so solemn I know it must be bad.

"What are you then?" I say, only because he expects me to ask. I don't want to know.

He shakes his head, and just that—I know he's about to tell me the truth. Maybe that's the worst, because I can't reciprocate.

He turns to me and fingers a lock of my hair. "Honey."

I swallow, ashamed. "That's not my real name. It's a lie."

"It's who you are to me," he murmurs, and in that one sentence I hear everything I am to him—someone to fuck, someone to protect. Someone to care for. His isn't the expression of a man who wants to convince me of something. His jaw is tense, eyes dark with regret. He'd rather be telling me anything but this—anything but the truth.

I remember what Candy said to me. *Dangerous.* Yes, he's dangerous. You only have to look at him to know. He's lethal energy in leather boots. He's a force of nature on a goddamn motorcycle. The question isn't whether he's dangerous. It's whether he's dangerous to me. "Are you going to hurt me?"

"No," he says, absolutely sure. Sure enough that it slaps me. Sure enough that I know he's considered doing it. "I'm going to help you through this."

Suspicion is acid down my throat. "Help me through *what?*"

His expression darkens. "I know who you're running from."

"Excuse me?" I laugh, unsteady. I don't want to believe him. "And anyway, it's not one person I'm running from. It's an army of them."

"Even better," he says. "I'm a soldier."

Two klicks to the south, he said when we got here. That's military terminology. I imagine him with his hair

149

less scruffy, his mouth clean shaven. I imagine him without the leather jacket or the bike, but instead in a uniform. He'd look good like that.

I'm guessing he *did* look good like that. I feel sick. "You used to be in the military?"

"Army," he confirms.

I remember the feeling I had that first night, that a cop was in the building. A man with military training. Exactly the kind of men my father and Byron hired as muscle.

The dangerous kind.

I take a step back. "Are you a cop?"

"No," he says grimly. "I have other things in common with Byron, but not that."

It's a slap to hear him say the name. It's real now.

I stare at him. A man with military training who shows up at the club. The first thing he does is ask for me. A private dance. He doesn't just watch me or fuck me. He wants to *talk.* He wants to know me. I'd thought it was sweet. Instead it was a lie. Like my name.

Like my whole fucking life.

I take another step back. I'm running away again, in slow motion this time. Part of me doesn't want to leave. I remember what Blue said about him—*the killing game.* "You're...what? A bounty hunter? A hired gun?"

"Something like that."

Sent to find me, to capture me. To hunt me down like an animal. "Is that why you stood up to Ivan? You didn't want someone else to get your prize?"

"No." His eyes are tortured.

"Tell me you didn't fuck me to get close." My throat is raw. My whole body is raw. "Tell me I'm wrong."

"You're not wrong," he says, his voice hoarse.

God. It makes me want to lash out. Push him away. How did he get so close?

"Is this what you always do?" My voice is thin, like a whip. I throw all my weight behind it, however little it may be. "Do you fuck every girl before you fuck her over? Maybe if the orgasm is good enough, they're more likely to go with you when you drag them back."

"I've never gone after a woman before. I never would have."

"Then why did you?"

He doesn't answer. His eyes are narrow, lips press together.

"Why me?" I'm shouting now. Hysterical. "How did I get so lucky?"

"Because of Byron," he says roughly. "I knew he was after you. And I had to see for myself. I had to... Not for any kind of fucking bounty. He's my brother. That's fucking why."

My heart is beating out of my chest, a wild thing. *No.*

Of course. Kip's mother, the incurable romantic. The lover of poetry. She named one son after Lord Byron and the other after Rudyard Kipling. The man who hurt me, abused me. And the man who helped me.

Or so I thought. But actually Kip is just part of the

family business—fucking me over.

"Your last name," I say, my voice raw.

"Adams."

Of course. That's what my last name would have been if I'd married Byron.

Now it's suddenly clear why I never got close to Kip. Never close enough to learn his last name. He never would have let me. He had to push me away. All those times he turned hot to cold, all those times the brambles and thorns pushed me out, he had a purpose.

"Any sisters I should know about?" I ask, the reality still sinking in. Kip and Byron. *Brothers.* "Any Emilys or Sylvias I should know about?"

He turns away, but not before I see him flinch. Then there is only his profile, stony and silhouetted by the pale light behind him.

When he faces me again, he has himself under control. Packed tightly under a veneer of determination and devil-may-care. Under raw power and lust. Deep down, there is some part of him that feels pain. Some part of him like me. That's not the part who's staring back at me now.

"Did he send you?" I ask, my voice small.

"Not exactly."

"But you're going to take me to him."

He pauses. "Yes."

Now it's my turn to flinch. I don't hide my face though, don't look away. I let him see how it makes me feel—cheap and hollow. I am a doll, with plastic makeup and real hair, made for men to play with. It hurts more than I could have thought. I'd imagined being caught by Byron. Or by one of his men. It had never been like this. It had never been betrayal.

"So what happens now?" I ask, empty. "You bring me to Byron and what? You both fuck me at the same time? Is that the endgame?"

"I'm not going to hurt you," he says with such quiet determination I almost believe him.

"You already are."

That's when the shooting starts.

Chapter Fourteen

GLASS SHATTERS.

I almost don't register what's happening, but Kip shouts at me. "Get down."

He doesn't wait to see if I obey. He pushes me down onto the floor, covering me with his body. I press my face into the floor. My brain is in a state of shock. All I can feel is the heaviness of his body, the heat of him. The grit on the floor. It shouldn't even matter now, but I can't help but wonder about that. Wasn't the floor smooth before? I was dancing just two minutes ago. It feels surreal. I was happy two minutes ago.

I believed that Kip would protect me—two minutes ago.

Then I realize this isn't grit, isn't bits of concrete crumbled off the ground. It's tiny shards of glass, and they're cutting into my cheek.

That's enough to snap me back into reality. I'm in danger. Someone is *shooting* at us.

"Who are they?" I ask even though it seems fairly obvious. More bounty hunters. More mercenaries. More killers. But why would they be shooting at Kip? He's one of them.

"We have to get out of here," Kip yells. "There's no cover."

He's right. The thin columns are no protection at all. He pulls me out of the ballroom. I stumble, but he catches me, shielding me with his body as grass explodes in fireworks at our feet.

He's holding something. What is it? Moonlight glints off a smooth black barrel.

A gun.

Why does he have a gun? Was he planning on shooting me? But no, then he couldn't bring me back to his brother—a living prize. I force down a sob. I have to run now. I have to survive. Like walking onto a blinding stage. Like running through gunfire.

Kip shoots back and that gives us a chance to get to the bike. I don't have time to think.

Only this. Only running.

We make it to his motorcycle and hop on. Then we're making a cloud of dust and disappearing down the lane. My heart pounds, louder than the engine. I cling to him, holding him tight in my arms, pressing my body against his as we put feet and yards and miles between us and them.

I know I can't trust him. I know that now more than ever, but for these minutes I don't have a choice. I couldn't stay back there and get shot at. I can't jump off a speeding motorcycle. It's completely without consent that I breathe in his leathery, clean-sweat scent. It's totally against my will that I lean into him, drawing strength from him.

We go back the way we came, the line of trees giving way to dark buildings and locked doors. My mind races with what just happened, but it's too loud to talk on here. The wind is a howl in my ears. It's like being underwater. We aren't driving; we're swimming, kicking up from the bottom, hoping we reach the surface in time.

I'm out of breath when he stops the bike. The panic hasn't slowed one bit. If anything, racing through the roads has me high on adrenaline. And fear.

"Don't touch me," I say. "Don't touch me. Don't touch me."

His eyes reflect concern, but he isn't glancing around wildly, isn't ducking behind a building. No, that's me, and he looks worried about that. He circles the bike and takes me in his arms.

"Hey." He pulls me into his chest, and I turn my face against him. A kiss lands on the crown of my head. "You're okay now. You're okay."

But I'm not. I can't outrun a bullet. I can't outrun a motorcycle.

I can't outrun *him*.

Tears are running down my cheeks. I feel out of control. "Why would they shoot us? I figured they'd want us back alive if they're going to get their money. Or did Byron just put out a hit on us."

"I need you to trust me now," Kip says.

I shake my head. There's no way. Trust? He's lost the

right to that.

And to be honest, I wouldn't even know how.

So I don't tell him the truth. I tell him a joke instead. That's what it is. "Honor," I say with a watery laugh. "That's my name. Honor."

And then I can't stop laughing, because that's how funny it is. A stripper named Honor.

My mother must have had such high hopes for me, to name me that. What did she think I would do with this life? Who did she think I would be? The laughing feels like crying, and I still can't stop.

I paint his T-shirt a dark gray, sticking it to his broad chest with my tears. I move him this way, whole sobs that shake my shoulders—and him too. I hate him but I let him comfort him me. He runs his hand down my hair, murmuring soothing words I can't understand. They don't matter anyway. I'm not Honor. I stopped being her the day I took my clothes off on that stage.

I'm Honey now.

Like the Grand—once beautiful, once strong. Built for greatness.

And now just a seedy strip club.

I wipe tears from my eyes. They come fast enough not to matter. My hands are wet with them. My cheeks too. "But you already knew my name, didn't you?"

He doesn't answer. But of course he's always known. He was already in on the joke.

✧   ✧   ✧

THE PLACE HE brings me to is a house. A nice house in a quiet old neighborhood with faded paint and well-trimmed lawns. Modest but well-cared for. It doesn't have the off-kilter charm of the Tropicana or the old-world allure of the Grand. This place is a home—only a few streets over from where I strip and hide. We're pressed together in the city.

I back away from him, down the driveway. I need to get to Clara.

And most of all, I need to get away from *him*.

He catches my arm. "It's not safe on the streets right now."

"And I'm safe with you?"

His expression is dark. "Maybe not. But you don't have a choice."

He pulls me toward the door. I go with him—not that I have a choice. He's stronger than me. Have I been trained not to fight that well? I feel numb. In shock. My arms and legs are wobbly. I'd fall if he didn't propel me along. He props me against the wall and glances along the street before shutting the door and locking it.

It feels like we are in the middle of a battle, only I don't have a weapon. My gaze flicks to my bag, which I dropped by the door.

The Taser.

"Don't take me to Byron," I say, almost begging, even though it's a lost cause. The shooters at the ballroom prove I've already been found by other mercenaries. And Kip—he's Byron's brother. Of all people, I understand the hold that family has on us. "Don't tell him you found me. Just let me go. I'll run. I'll—"

His eyes are so dark, almost angry as they take me in. He reaches up, and I flinch. His hand freezes an inch from my face. "He hurt you."

"No," I say too quickly. I don't want Kip to know what his brother did. God, even I don't want to know. If I could scrub it from my mind, I would. If I could take a scalpel and carve the memories out, I would. I'll never let that happen to Clara, not ever.

"From the glass," he says gently. "You're bleeding."

Oh. And sure enough, when I reach up, my fingers come away smeared with red.

I must still be in shock, because I'm standing there, staring at my blood like I've never seen it before. In fact I've seen my blood plenty of times. And cuts and bruises. We're old friends. "It's nothing," I say. "I can't feel anything."

"It's not nothing. Let me take care of you." It sounds broader when he says it, like he's talking about more than the cuts on my face.

"I don't need anything *from you.*"

His eyes are dark, accepting my accusations. But not my answer. "Wait here."

"Kip, please. Let me go. I need to go…"

"To your sister?" he asks softly. It's not really a question though.

Dread is a cold stone in my stomach. "You can't

touch her. You can't—"

"I'm not going to do anything to her."

"So you can turn us in for whatever price is on our head?"

"It's not about the fucking money."

I smile grimly. "It's always about the money."

He grasps my chin, careful not to push the glass in deeper. He manages not to touch my cuts at all. But his look is just as sharp. "I'm not going to give you to Byron. But I am going to use you. To put a stop to this. To end it."

"How?" I whisper. There are a lot of ways this can end.

I don't come out alive in most of them.

He shakes his head. "I'm not sure yet. And with Byron's men in Tanglewood, we don't have much time. So I need you to trust me. I need you to sit down and wait. I need you to let me pull the fucking glass out of your face."

Then he's stalking toward the hallway, presumably to get bandages or tweezers.

It's a command, and I've been trained all my life to obey. Still, I remain standing. Could I make it back to the Tropicana from here? I know we're close enough, but I haven't explored enough to be sure of the way. Abruptly I sit on his couch, shaking. *Clara.*

Kip could help us. He has a gun. He used it to protect me.

I need you to trust me.

A clock points to four thirty. Still morning. *Still night.* I'm cutting it close getting back to her. If she's even there, she'd be leaving soon. But then, maybe it's better that way. If she's safe now, she might stay that way. Better than me going back, leading those shooters right to our doorstep.

I ignore the pang in my chest at the thought of never seeing her again. *Safe.*

There is a book on the side table. I recognize it even though I've never seen it before. Rudyard Kipling's book of stories, the ones Kip told me about. This book looks ancient, its pages well touched, both soft and brittle in the way old things sometimes are. I flip open the cover, feeling like I'm intruding on something private. This whole night has been intrusion—me, him, this book that is his namesake.

There's something written in faded black ink on the first page. Not printed with the book but added after. It's a poem.

The jungle is a scary place for those who wander in

It holds its secrets tightly furled, locking out the wind

Each leaf has a map, each river points the way

But the jungle is too good a host.

Y)u really must stay.

So lay your body on the dirt,

And make not a sound.

Only when you rest you'll find,

The key is underground.

I read the poem again, imagining walking into a forest. Being afraid and lost. It's not a foreign feeling even though I've rarely left the city. The jungle is where I lived most of my life, in the mansion I wasn't allowed to leave, where the trees are made of marble, where the leaves are gilded gold. I may have finally broken my way out, but sometimes I wonder if that's an illusion. Maybe I'll wake up and find myself back there, that my time at the Grand was all a bad dream.

Or maybe I'll realize I died in that mansion, that freedom is just ghostly wishful thinking.

Kip comes back with tweezers and a bottle smelling of rubbing alcohol. He glances down at the book, a strange expression on his face.

"Did you write this?" I ask, gesturing to the poem.

He shakes his head. "My mother."

"Oh." I look again at the last line, the final escape from the jungle. *Underground.* She's talking about death. "It's pretty. And sad."

"That was my mother. Pretty and sad." He pours some of the rubbing alcohol on a cotton swab. "No more stalling now. I hate having to hurt you, but the sooner we start, the sooner we finish."

It's disturbing how like Byron he is… "Do what you have to do."

He sits beside me and places my hand on his thigh.

"When it hurts, squeeze."

He feels like a denim-covered log in my hand. "I don't think I'd be able to squeeze—oh shit, that hurts."

It turns out I have more hand strength than I realized, especially when a man with large, gentle hands carefully uses tweezers to extract glass shards from my face. I must be leaving five dents in his leg, even through his jeans, where my nails dig in. He doesn't flinch or jump, even when I hold on for dear life, even when I can't hold in a little whimper.

Little pieces of red glass line up on the towel he laid out.

"That'll stain," I whisper.

"Let it."

The couch is old but comfortable, lumpy in the way you can sink into. It's too feminine a house for Kip, though. Everything is rose gold and sunshine yellow, corduroy softness and old brass fixtures. And dust. The house doesn't feel lived in. Nothing like the hard man in leather and grit. "You grew up here?"

He doesn't answer. His lack of expression tells me he did. "I don't stay here much."

"Why are you here now, then? Is it just a convenient place to stay while you hunt me down?"

"If that was true, I would have taken you back to Nevada when I first met you."

"So why didn't you?"

He pauses after the next sliver and looks me in the eye. "It's complicated."

"This isn't a relationship status."

"We don't have a fucking relationship."

I suck in a breath. It's like he's slapped me. No, it's worse than that. It never hurt this much when Byron bent me over and fucked me dry.

Then his head lowers, before I'm even aware of what he might do. I'm braced for more pain. More lies. His lips are featherlight on mine. I hold still, allowing his mouth to move over mine, corner to corner, finding every square centimeter of my lips, kissing away the hurt.

When he reaches a little too close to my cheek, I can't help but flinch.

He pulls back, regret on his face. "We need to get moving."

"There is no *we*," I say softly. "You made that clear."

His eyes turn hard. "Let me finish cleaning your wounds. Then we'll go."

I'm looking at Kip, but all I can see are Byron's eyes, his nose, his mouth. My heart slams into my chest as I remember that face looming over me, fucking me. Hurting me. I don't know why I couldn't see it before. Of course they're brothers. They're the same.

I have to leave without him. I can't trust him at all. He's been kind to me at times, but he's also been rough and crude and cold. For all I know he will drag me back to Byron out of family loyalty. *Delitto d'onore*. An honor killing. That's what it will be.

I need to get out of here. I need to get away from him.

I can't trust him, even though I want to. *God, I want to.*

He leaves the room again to put away the supplies, and I know this is my chance.

I get the Taser he gave me and follow him into the bathroom. His eyes meet mine in the mirror. I smile that fake, seductive smile I've perfected through hours onstage. One hand slides up his back, meant to distract. To disarm.

He isn't fooled.

Something awful flashes through his eyes—recognition. He knows what's about to happen. And even worse—acceptance. He's strong enough, fast enough to stop me.

"Honor," he says.

Just that one word.

It's the first time he uses my real name, and I repay him by using the Taser on him. He knows he deserves it, and I know it too—but that doesn't make it any easier.

I press it to his side and press the trigger.

The shock reverberates up my arm. Kip falls like a tree, shaking the ground, falling against the door frame, body rocked by the powerful electric shock. It's Kip who's hurt, Kip who I leave on the floor.

I barely have time to whisper *I'm sorry* before I'm gone.

Chapter Fifteen

I PRACTICALLY RUN back toward the motel room, out of breath.

Even at full speed, hurdle jumping turned trash cans and puddles of dark liquid, I can't forget the way he looked, his big body hurting, incapacitated, at my hands. *Why do you care what happens to him?* Kip said that to me once. But I do care. Guilt is something I'm used to by now, but it doesn't get any easier.

I glance back, but the streets behind me are empty. No Kip. And no one else.

I run toward Clara, trying to make it back before she leaves.

Maybe she is better off running anyway. I can't get the thought out of my head. Like pushing a baby bird out of the nest because she needs to fly. But I can't do it. I can't let her go. Maybe that's my weakness. Maybe that's her downfall.

Or maybe I've learned lessons from my father too well.

That's what we do to the women we love, isn't it? We tuck them in a room, give them food and books, tell them to be happy. Sometimes it works. But other times the woman fucks a guard. Other times the woman doesn't like her fiancé's fists. Other times they run. Then what will you do?

I did the same thing to Clara as my father did to me. I locked her in a tower.

I take a long roundabout way back to the motel. If I see anyone, anything suspicious, I won't go back. I'd let myself be taken first. But the streets are empty. Barren.

Finally I let myself slip into the Tropicana from the back. The bricks are lit by Christmas lights, the palm trees dark and sinister. I pause in the little walkway between our building and the next. Something is different.

The Madonna. It's not in the window anymore. It's gone—and so is Clara.

Everything in me slows. My heart. My head. I even blink slower, eyelids dropping, blotting out the sight of that empty window. I'm swaying where I stand, off balance, and I don't care. That was our signal. If she was ever to run, she would take the Madonna with her. Then the wall is behind me, cool brick holding me up. I lean my head back and let the guilt and shame and sorrow wash over me.

There's gladness too. Relief that she's gone, away from me. She'll be safer without me.

Maybe I have always known she would be.

I hadn't been able to let Clara go, though. I loved her too much, needed her more than she knew. Or maybe she did know, because she fought me about leaving.

Every time she'd tell me no. But it looked like she listened to me anyway.

Dawn broke over the tallest buildings, rays fracturing around broken spires, bathing every crack in orange and pink. And she left, just like I told her to.

Kip can't get to her. He'll never find her.

And neither will I.

Something moves in the room. A brush against the drapes. They sway, just slightly. I wipe my tears so I can see more clearly. Is she still there? Have I caught her before she's left?

I take a step toward the room. Another.

"Clara?" I whisper.

The landlord wouldn't have started clearing out our room already. Clara wouldn't have stopped to tell him she was leaving. And anyway we're paid through the week. Cash, of course.

Then the door opens. A man stands in the doorway. I would recognize him anywhere. Hadn't he stood in the doorway to my room enough times, blocking me, frowning?

Daddy. This time I don't whisper. My lips move, but I don't make a sound.

He looks up anyway, right at me, where I stand in the shadows. He sees me. His body shifts, moves toward me. He is old now, with knees that ache, and back problems, but he was a warrior once. A killer.

He still is.

I run.

✦　✦　✦

SO MUCH FOR eighteen years of ballet lessons and long hours spent on the pole. He is old, but he is a born hunter. All I want is to get away. I run toward the Grand. Strange—I shouldn't feel safe there. But I do. He must have anticipated it, because he cuts me off in an alley.

A hand on my wrist, clamping down hard. "Honor!"

That hand had tucked me into bed. It had rested on my head while my fiancé fucked me over the desk.

That hand had killed my mother.

I'm holding the Taser but he's got my wrist. He squeezes—hard—and my grip loosens. The Taser clatters to the ground. My father kicks it into a pile of trash bags. Disappeared into the shadows and muck.

"Be still," he snaps.

"Did you take her?" I demand. I twist away, but I can't get free. "Did you take Clara?"

"She wasn't there. The room is empty."

I don't even know if I believe him. "Let me go. Just let me go."

Even though there's nowhere for me to go anymore. Not after the motel room has been found out and violated. I can only hope he's telling the truth about Clara being gone before he got there. Did she get some idea that they were on to us? Is that why she left, when she always swore she'd wait for me?

He wrests me back—and down. I fall onto the concrete, knees scraped in a blinding flash of pain. It's like going onstage. He leans over me, breathing hard, eyes wild. "Why did you leave?" he demands.

I laugh and shudder at the same time. The result is a broken sound. A cry. "You know."

"I didn't care if your sister was gone, but you—"

"And that's why I had to go. Because you didn't care about her." I wrench my hand away, but I'm kneeling now. I'm lost. We're in the middle of the sidewalk in the shitty part of town, but no one will interfere. No one would lift a hand to protect me. "You didn't care about me either. Not when you gave me to Byron."

His face is twisted in rage. Or guilt? "You should have come to me."

I laugh. Maybe it's the wrong thing to do in this moment. Lord knows I would never have laughed in my father's face back home, in the mansion, running across Aubusson rugs in my ballet slippers as if they could somehow transport me somewhere else.

We aren't in the mansion anymore. The ballet slippers did take me somewhere else. They gave me a way to support us as we ran. "You saw, Daddy." I'm bitter. And too tired to lie. "You saw what he did to me and patted my head. Like I was a *pet*."

"You are my *daughter*," he shouts, and the way he says it, it means the same thing.

"No, you're right," I say, sarcastic now. "I'm sure you would have protected me if I'd asked you to. You'd have protected me the same way you did my mother."

He grows still. His eyes narrow, and for the first time

since he's caught me, real fear slices through me. Even in the depths of my sorrow, my sister gone and my lover's betrayal, I don't want to die.

"What of Portia? I did not beat her."

"And that's the gold standard, is that right? What about a gun, did you shoot her? Or a knife—did you stab her?"

He reaches for me—my hair. He leans down, his hand tightening, tilting my head back. "What do you mean, bambina?" His words are low, silky. "Are you afraid of me?"

I'm trembling, panting. "Should I be?"

Abruptly he releases me. My head jerks with the impact, but I'm still kneeling, and I catch myself on my hands. Loose gravel slides under my palms, reminding me of the roof above the Grand.

"Of course not," he says. "I'm your father. We'll go back home. Everything will go back to the way it was."

It can never go back to the way it was. Not only because I don't have Clara now. I'm changed too. Dancing at the Grand has changed me. Kip changed me.

Oh God, Kip.

If I go with my father now, I'll never see Kip again. And that's a good thing. He's a bastard, just like he told me he is. I have the strangest thought that I should have let him bring me in. At least then he'd get the bounty on my head. After all his work finding me...fucking me...

A tear rolls down my cheek.

"There now," my father says, pulling me up by my

arm. "Everything will be okay. You don't have to stay here anymore."

That's why he thinks I'm crying. Because I don't want to live in this motel. What he doesn't know is I'd give anything to go back to the way things were a week ago. Clara and I safely in the motel. And me walking with Kip after work, having no idea he was only there to betray me.

Maybe it could have been enough, to return to that life. If only. "Why did you kill her?" I whisper.

"Portia?" He shakes his head. "I don't know where you got this idea, bambina. I would have killed her. Should have, maybe. But I never hurt one hair on her pretty head."

"You expect me to believe her death was an accident? The wife of a mafioso, an accident?"

He looks sad suddenly. And incredibly old. I can see in him the pain in his joints and his back from chasing me. I can see the toll these months have taken on him, searching for me—missing me? "I never told you the truth. I thought I was protecting you. But maybe I was only protecting myself."

I swallow hard to hear him admit it. "Then you did kill her."

Pain flashes through his eyes. "I didn't kill her. No one did."

"Liar," I say, shaking with fury.

There's no way she's alive. That was just a childish dream.

And I think, I won't need a Taser to bring a man down. A swift, hard kick to the nuts can do that. And God, my legs are strong. My thighs are fucking weapons after dancing onstage every night. I left my father on the ground. I am practically a black widow, leaving men broken and in pain wherever I go. In those seconds I feel powerful.

And then he says something that is my downfall. "I won't let Byron touch you again," my father says. "I shouldn't have let him touch you at all."

It was what I always wanted from him. Protection. Caring. I guess a little girl never stops wanting her daddy. But mine is just an illusion. I know, because a second later Byron appears behind him.

I would have expected him to grow scarier in my mind, as if my fears could morph him into a monster. But he seems almost more sinister in that suit and that smile, cat got the cream. "You found her."

My father's hand tightens on me. He turns halfway, caught between us. "Byron. I need a moment with my daughter. Then we'll talk."

He advances on us, and both my father and I shrink back. There is a new confidence to the man. I'm assuming it has something to do with the gang of muscle-bound men behind Byron, armed and cold. Mercenaries.

"The time for talking is over," Byron says. "And so is your usefulness. I'm sorry your daughter shot you, though. That's a rough way to go."

I scream and yank my father down, but Byron is fast. His aim is perfect. He blows a hole in my father's head, and the blood spatters on my hands.

CHAPTER SIXTEEN

YOU HAVE TO look on the bright side. I learned that early. There's always a bright side. In this case, the bright side is that Clara definitely got away safe. If I wasn't sure before, now I know she's definitely gone. Her books are missing, and the Madonna is gone too.

And I know Byron doesn't have her. Because he's torturing me trying to find her.

It's such a relief that I have no fucking clue where she is.

Thwack.

I can't be sure I wouldn't give her up. I love her more than anything. More than my life, not that it's worth much. I would gladly die for her, but the thing about death is, it's not easy. Not when I'm tied up in a motel room. I can't exactly swallow some pills I don't have or slit my wrists when they're tied down with rope. I can only endure every strike of Byron's belt. I can only survive.

Thwack. Thwack. Thwack.

Two of the men sit at the table where Clara and I ate meals together. I have the unsettling feeling they are waiting for Byron to be finished with me. That they are

175

waiting for their turns.

"Where is she?" Byron says. I almost think he knows I don't have the answer. I think he doesn't care.

I shake my head.

Thwack.

My body jerks in the bonds. I'm tied at both wrists and ankles, face up. The whole bed shakes with the impact. And the pain…God, the pain is unbearable. It's blinding. It's all the lights onstage and all the hands touching me. It's a snake bite, the lash of the tail and the sting of the teeth biting into my flesh.

But I have to bear it. Death isn't easy. I can only survive.

Thwack.

I have more empathy for Candy than I could have before. If she's felt even a fraction of this pain, no wonder she shoots up. I'd do anything to feel numb.

"Please," I whimper.

I didn't mean to say it. Didn't mean to beg. He doesn't deserve the satisfaction.

He does pause. He sets the belt on the bed. The mattress groans as he leans down toward me. "What was that?" he says, his voice deceptively gentle.

There are more men waiting outside, standing watch. I wonder if they've bothered to clear out the whole motel. It might be safer, just to make sure there are no witnesses. On the other hand, why bother? No one will have seen anything by the time the police come through. And if they did, Byron's friends' connections would cover it up.

"I don't know where she is," I whisper.

He leans closer, his mouth just inches from my ear. "Why should I believe you?"

I taste something metallic on my tongue. Blood? "Because I'm telling the truth."

He leans back, smiling. "I'm not in a hurry, sweetheart. I've been waiting a long time to get my hands on you again. I intend to savor this. You'll be praying for death before I'm done with you."

What he doesn't understand is that I'm already praying for death. I've lost everything.

My sister. I'll never see her again.

Thwack.

And Kip. God, he was never really mine. But the hope of him was so sweet.

Thwack.

Even my father. I had waited so long for him to stand up for me. Did he mean it about my mother? That would mean he didn't kill her.

Thwack.

But if she's been alive all this time, it means she left me. Abandoned me to this life.

Thwack thwack thwack.

It's too much. The physical pain. The emotional. My soul is on fire. My skin is ablaze. The edges of my vision turn crimson.

Byron looms over me, a smile on his face. And I am more afraid than ever. It's never good when he's pleased.

"I know what you've been doing here. A stripper. Fuck, I'm glad I didn't marry you. I'd have had to kill you. I guess I'll kill you either way."

Don't let him get to you. He can fuck with my body, but I don't want him to fuck with my mind. I have a sick feeling he'll do both, and I won't be able to stop him.

"I know about your little boyfriend too."

My stomach turns over. "Your brother?"

Byron laughs, and dread settles deep into my core. "I'm surprised he told you about that." There's a gleam in Byron's eye. "Did he tell you our family secrets too?"

A little. I know about Kip's father and how he left them. I knew they grew up poor. Is that why Byron seemed to hate me from the beginning, because my family had money? "No."

"The fucking jewels. They belong to my family. To me. I thought they were gone...but then you came here." He leans close. "Where are they?"

"I don't know."

"Don't know where the jewels are. Don't know where your sister is." He snorts in disgust. "You're not much use to me, are you?"

"Then let me go."

"You were going to be my consolation prize. You and your father's entire fucking empire. Did you know that? I couldn't have the jewels, but I could have everything else." He runs a finger over my breast, taking my nipple between thumb and forefinger. Rolling. Squeezing. "And you were my little jewel, weren't you? I polished you, didn't I?"

A tear rolls down the side of my face. "No," I choke out, but it's a lie.

Because he did polish me, until I shined, until I was both flat and sharp. He used me like a jewel—a thing to be worn and then tossed into a drawer.

"Not just you, Honor. You weren't the only jewel in my crown." His hand circles my throat. "Did Kip tell you about our sister?"

My breath catches. *Any Emilys or Sylvias I should know about?* But he never answered.

"She grew up different than us. She had all the things we never did."

Suspicion is a dark vine wrapped around my lungs. Making it hard to breathe. Two poor brothers. A sister who grew up rich. It seems impossible. I'm praying it's not true. I'm praying it's not *me.*

His hand on my neck squeezes, cutting off my air supply. "Her name is Clara," he whispers.

And I black out.

✧   ✧   ✧

WHEN I WAKE up again, it's dark. There is a man sitting beside me. I recognize him from the dining table earlier. He is one of Byron's men. He runs his hand up and down my belly, occasionally cupping my breast, kneading me. I don't know how long he's been doing that. My skin crawls. He brushes over a welt from earlier, and I gasp.

He looks startled—then amused. "You're awake."

My mind is still spinning from what I know. Kip. Byron. Clara. All of them, related.

And me too.

It all makes sense now, in a horrible way.

The hand tightens on my breast until I whimper. The other man from the table is leaning against the wall, watching. Both of them are dangerous, but the one on the wall scares me more. There's something flat in his eyes. Something reptilian.

In the time that passed, the rope has loosened—just slightly. There's more give than before. But I'm still not sure I could pull my hand free without breaking it. And if I did get free, there'd be nowhere to go. They'd just tie me up tighter. They'd just hurt me more.

The first man runs his hand over my body, poking at the bruises already formed, reaching down between my legs and shoving into my dry pussy. "Awake and ready for us."

I'm not ready for anything they'll do to me.

The bathroom door swings open, drawing a triangle of light onto the thin carpet. *Byron.* I never thought I'd be relieved to see him. But instead of coming to the bed, he goes and takes one of the empty chairs at the table. He crosses one leg over the other, settling in. His Italian shoes shine even in the dim light. His suit is custom-tailored.

From across the room he smirks at me. He speaks to his men but never breaks eye contact with me. "Find out where her sister went. I don't care what you have to do to get her to talk."

The man sitting beside me nods in greedy assent. His hands grow rougher. They aren't torture, except the emotional kind. The same kind of shame I lived every night on that stage. I get the sense he wants to fuck me more than hurt me, though I'm sure he'll do both before the night is up.

The sound of a zipper rends the air. The man by the wall hasn't moved from his position except to lower his fly and take out his cock. He's stroking himself, watching.

You were going to be my consolation prize.

I brace myself, trying to clear my mind. Like in the moments behind the curtain, waiting to go onstage. Like the moments when I hid outside my father's study, listening to him order a hit, dying a little inside.

There's no escape. Even death is closed off to me on this bed.

A knock comes at the door. I close my eyes, wondering how many minutes this will buy me. It will be one of Byron's men, of course, maybe with a perimeter-check update. Or maybe they're delivering coffee. The men in his employ are nothing more than lackeys on steroids.

The man by the wall doesn't stop watching me, doesn't stop stroking.

Of course Byron wouldn't bother himself to get up, not when someone else could do it. That leaves the man touching me. He looks disgruntled to have to stop, but he's not going to complain out loud. With one regretful pinch of my nipple, he stands and goes to the door. He's not afraid here, surrounded by his own men, protected by a goddamn battalion's worth of firepower in one tiny broke-down motel. He doesn't check the peephole, he just swings the door open—and takes a bullet to the chest.

I stare at him, unable to comprehend what happened. Byron stares too, frozen for one sweet moment of victory. But from his position he can see out the door, and whatever he sees makes him snarl. He pulls out his gun and dives for the bathroom, taking cover as the shooting starts.

The man by the wall is the slowest to react. I guess stroking your hard-on can slow a guy down.

But he is also the most lethal. The least human.

When he realizes they're under attack, he doesn't even bother putting his dick away. He just whips out his gun and starts shooting, without a visual, his erection waving, unprotected. I yank at the straps tying me down. This is my chance to get away. I don't know what's happening—if this is some kind of fighting within the ranks—but I have to use this.

The bonds are too tight. No matter how I pull them, they only get tighter.

My muscles burn under the strain. Every yank makes the bruises and welts on my stomach and breasts ache. I'm trapped here in the middle of a fucking gunfight, completely naked. Even more exposed than the guy edging along the wall, gun at the ready, dick out.

He steps out to make his shot and takes a hit. His body ricochets back, falling to the ground. He's been clipped at the side. Blood sprays. The attacker steps into the room and gives him another shot—this one to the knee.

The man steps forward, and the light from the bathroom hits his face. *Kip.*

His eyes are wild. He's a goddamn gladiator like this, more animal than human, more fierce than merciful. He takes in my nakedness on the bed. Then he looks at the man writhing and gurgling on the floor at his feet. It's not hard to see what's happening here, and Kip reacts quickly—faster than I could have. He shoves his boot against the man's exposed, limp dick and turns his heel. There is an awful, high-pitched primal sound of pain that is abruptly cut off by a final gunshot to the head.

My mind can barely catch up with what he's done. He's taken on two of Byron's men—and won. No, he must have taken on even more of them, the ones patrolling outside. The ones who had been incapacitated, or dead, when he strolled up and knocked on the door, catching these men unaware.

He's incredible. He's a monster. I'm going to throw up. And with nowhere to go, no way to move, I'd choke on my own vomit.

Kip isn't safe yet though. I try to tell him. "Bathroom," I yell, but it only comes out as a wheeze.

It's all right though. He seems to already know. His

gun is pointed toward the open door, waiting to take his shot. But Byron didn't get to be where he is by accident. He's not only a fucking good criminal. He's also a cop. "You don't want to do this, Kip," he calls. "Turn yourself in now and it will go easier for you."

Kip shakes his head. "This is much easier."

"You may have gotten through them, but you'll never take me. You won't make it out of this room alive." There's a pause, and his tone changes. "Unless we work together, like the old days. I know you have a thing for the girl. We can work it out. You can have her."

Kip glances at me, and for one awful moment I wonder if he'll go along with whatever horrible thing Byron plans to do to me. Then Kip's eyes darken at the welts on my skin, and I know he would never do anything to hurt me. He's here to save me. But Byron must have expected me to distract him, because he takes the opportunity to pop out of the bathroom and fire off a round.

Kip dives to cover my body with his, shooting back.

The thing about a bullet is, it doesn't feel like fire after all. Maybe I'm numb from being tied up too long. It feels like ice instead. I'm hit, I realize. Hit in the side.

Be careful, I wish I could say. *He doesn't fight fair.* No one does. Not Byron, not Kip. Not even me.

I fought as dirty as possible, keeping Clara away from Byron, keeping her safe—and I succeeded. This is the jungle, and only the fittest survive. Though I may not be very fit anymore, because I feel myself fading. Falling. Thank goodness for the rope around my wrists. Otherwise I'd sink down beneath the ground.

Instead I'm suspended, waiting.

There's shooting back and forth—all around. That much I can tell from the blasts to my eardrums. But Kip is trapped. I'm the one tied up, but he's the one in a vulnerable position—right in front of me. He can't duck behind the bed where he'd be safe. I think he can't even storm the bathroom because that would leave me exposed. The only cover he has is the second bed. He's using it to protect himself—and shooting whenever Byron tries to aim out, so he's forced to retreat. It won't last for long though.

He's going to get himself killed, and it will be my fault. Mine. *I can't let that happen.*

I force myself back to reality. I'd been slipping before. The pain and shock of it had let me drift in a kind of unreality. But now I'm fully aware of every bruise and cut on my skin, acutely aware of how much I hurt. I pull my hand where it's tied—nothing happens. The rope may have more give, but it's still tight enough I can't pull my hand out.

I pull again, harder, twisting myself, as the bullets ricochet off the wall. One lands in the mattress underneath me, snapping a coil with a loud *twang*. Any second now one will hit Kip. He's still blocking me. *Still protecting me.*

The hole is too small. It's like I'd have to break my hand to get it out.

Something settles over me. Confidence. Recklessness.

Sometimes they're the same thing. So let my hand break. It's a hard thing to break your own hand, in the same way that it can be hard to die. I have to let go of the survival instinct. I have to break myself.

I pull, using all my strength, straining at my ankles to build this much force. The bed creaks.

Something in my hand snaps.

Now my left hand is free. That gives me enough room to un-loop the rope from the pole, so my right hand is free. My left hand is messed up—broken?—but my right hand still works. I jerk myself up, unsteady on my feet.

And fall, stumbling to the ground. It's safer here.

"Stay down," Kip orders before firing off a round.

Safety doesn't matter anymore.

If anyone will get shot, it will be Kip. He matters.

I crawl to one of the men on the floor and take his gun.

The thing about men is they always underestimate me. Because I'm small and weak. Because I have a pussy instead of a cock. And my father, he kept me locked up. For all those reasons, I am ill-equipped for the world. But one thing I know is violence. I've been around violent men all my life. I've been around them when they pulled out their guns, when they flicked off the safety. Been around them when they fired. And I was watching.

I aim and fire. The kick is enough to knock me backward, but there's a brand-new hole in the wall courtesy of me.

And I have Byron's attention. He's smirking, of

course.

So I walk toward him. Kip lunges for me, but I'm expecting that. I evade him and go toward Byron. I know I don't have the aim to hit him far away. I don't have months or years of target practice. And my hand is possibly broken. It feels like it's on fire. But if I'm close, I can get him.

That assumes he won't shoot me first. He could. At this point I wouldn't mind much. But I don't think he will. Because he underestimates me most of all.

We're one foot away now. Kip is right behind me, about to expose himself, make himself vulnerable to save me. I can't let that happen.

I aim the gun at Byron. Now he's the one looking down the barrel. He's the one counting.

"You wouldn't," he says coldly. Confidently. Not counting, after all.

I fire. I'm aiming for the center of his chest. The kickback from the gun and wrenching pain in my hand means I hit his shoulder instead. And it feels good. After all the times he slapped me, fucked me. Hurt me. God, my hand hurts. But it feels really good too. *Sweet victory.*

Though it doesn't feel exactly like victory when he manages to grab me. He spins me around and puts a gun to my head.

He wants to use me as a hostage. And it's already working. I see Kip's eyes dark with anger—and fear. He's afraid for me, because there's a gun to my head. But I've already broken my own hand. I'm fucking invincible. He's pointing his gun at us both, but I know he won't shoot. He can't, not without hitting me too.

"Hello, little brother," Byron says, and that's enough to shock me out of my plan.

Kip nods slightly. "I wish I could say I was glad to see you."

Byron laughs. "Aren't you? You've been searching for me for weeks."

"Not you. Her."

"Ah yes." Byron looks down at me, moving the nozzle of the gun to my side. "She's a good fuck. But not worth all this trouble if you ask me. Girls like that, they're a dime a dozen."

Kip looks furious. His nostrils flare. He's probably going to say something to defend me. Or maybe he'll just start shooting. I don't give him the chance. Because I can defend myself.

I'm only Byron's captive if I want to survive. I'm done surviving.

I reach down and grab the gun. He could have fought me if I tried to take it from him. I don't. Instead I squeeze the trigger. I shoot myself. I cinch the trap. He doesn't have anything left to bargain with now. He doesn't even have my body to shield himself. I fall to the floor, and I hear the shots that kill Byron—one, two, three—before he collapses beside me.

Then Kip is there, turning me over, pressing a hand to my side, swearing and praying and pleading. "God, Honor. Why did you—Jesus. Please live. Please keep her alive. God, please."

Chapter Seventeen

IT FEELS LIKE a dream.

I'm underwater. Lights and shadows dance in front of my eyes. Everything is muted, even the pain. But it's there. And voices. I recognize that voice. She's not talking to me, though. She's far away.

"Clara," I say, but it comes out like a croak. A rough sound, like rocks tumbling over each other.

She hears me anyway.

"Go back to sleep," she says, and something cool and soft brushes over my forehead. It feels important, her saying that. It feels important the way she's taking care of me, keeping me safe. Isn't that my job?

Safe.

I have to make sure she's safe. I fight against the water, but it's so heavy and thick. The only things I can see are a sterile white ceiling. The only thing I can smell is the sharp tang of cleaning solution. I'm in a hospital bed.

"Everything's fine." Her voice is soothing. "Just rest."

But I can't rest if I'm worried about her. I could never rest. *So tired.* "Are you okay?" The words are still garbled but she answers me.

"I'm fine. And you are too. We made it out okay, because of you."

Only then can I relax again. Only then can I breathe.

It's like breaking the surface, coming up for air. *Safe.*

Her hand grasps mine, warm where I'm cold. I soak in her heat, basking in the rays of her. "I know you're hurting," she says softly. And even in my delirium I know she isn't just talking about the physical pain. She's talking about every cold glance on my body and every cruel word. She's talking about being afraid. And I am afraid, just not for the same reasons I was before.

"Kip?" I ask, my voice rough.

"He's not here right now. If you wait a minute I can—"

But the pull of the drugs and the pain and the tiredness are too strong. They drag me under, like an anchor tied to my ankles. I sink to the bottom, barely aware. I only know one thing. I may have lost Kip. I may not have ever really had him. But I have Clara back.

I set her free.

Chapter Eighteen

I WAKE UP like coming up for air—suddenly and with a jolt. I'm upright in a bed, and there's an ache in my side. The bullet. Byron. *Kip*.

It comes back to me in a rush, and I lie back down in the bed.

Close my eyes.

Wish I could be asleep again.

That ship has sailed. I peek one eye open and look around at the pale yellow curtains and the painting of ballet dancers on a barre. The floor is the color of cinnamon, the walls a soft taupe. The elements of the room chatter together, that's how it feels. They're friends and confidantes of each other, and my presence here feels intimate, not intrusive.

I'm not sure how much time passes like that, drifting, communing with doorknobs and drywall. I turn my head and face the window—and then I see it. Silhouetted by the orange glow is the Madonna from our motel room.

"Clara," I whisper.

Something moves from the corner of the room. *Kip*.

My head is still a little woozy from whatever drugs I

have in me, but I would recognize him anywhere. Even though he looks rougher for the wear, his eyes shadowed, his scruff darker. He's blinking away sleep just like I am, except he was on a hard chair in the corner, and I was on the bed.

"You're up," he says, his voice gruff. "It's time for another dose."

"No." I shake my head, ignoring the pain even that small movement causes. My hand is aching and bandaged. My side is on fire. "No drugs."

His expression is stern. "It's medicine for the pain. You can take two pills every six hours, and it's been—"

"I don't want it. At least, not right now." I have to speak slowly, carefully, but I'm gaining more focus with every word I say. I have hazy memories of a hospital bed with thin sheets and a warm, strong hand holding mine. I remember being discharged and coming here... Has he been taking care of me?

It's all too unreal, like something I dreamed instead of lived. That's the drugs.

He doesn't look thrilled about the deviation from my schedule. "You're in pain," he says flatly.

"I'll live."

No smile either. "Honor—"

"Oh, I'm Honor now? I thought you liked me better as Honey."

Pain flashes over his face. "You were shot a week ago. You need rest. You need to take your pills."

A week? How many more days will I lose if I swallow

more pills? No. No more delays. I went too long without knowing the truth. Especially the truth about him. I can deal with a lot of bad things. Hell, everyone has a past. Including me. But I need answers now. I need to know.

"Where's Clara?"

He meets my gaze. "She's here. She's safe."

Relief is cool and wide, an open space so I can breathe again. "And she's your sister?"

His eyes are solemn. "Yes."

So what does that make us? "Tell me everything."

He runs a hand through his hair and blows out a breath. "Okay. That's fair. But before I tell you that…" He paces away and comes back. "Just know I'm not proud of what I did. Maybe I had my reasons. Like being a selfish bastard. That's a reason. But I'm not proud."

I already feel sick to my stomach just thinking of it, and I've only been conscious for a few minutes. "You told me the story of how the tiger got his stripes. Now tell me how you got yours."

I'm asking for more than the story of his tattoos. I'm asking for his life, his pain.

I deserve that much.

He sits on the edge of the bed and takes my hand in his.

"I told you my father left us, my mother and me," he begins. "What I didn't say is that he left to be with another woman. He worked security for a wealthy family. He had an affair with the woman. They ran away together."

I didn't kill her. No one did. She's still alive. "My mother."

He hesitates. Then nods. "Yes."

"But you and I aren't..."

Kip's brow furrows. "Related? No."

"Thank God." I hadn't thought so because of the timeline. But then I hadn't thought Kip was Clara's half-brother either. It feels damn good to be sure...

A ghost of a smile brushes over his lips. "Clara is your half-sister. And she's my half-sister. If our parents had managed to get married, that would make us stepsiblings. But they didn't. And so we're nothing."

Nothing. The word clangs in my hollow chest.

Maybe he feels the loss too, because he paces away and then walks back. He runs a hand over his face. Every anxious movement increases my fear tenfold. I thought I was safe now. The monster was slain—both my father and Byron. I'm out of my childhood mansion. I'm no longer in the Grand. I've escaped everything I've ever been running from. Only I don't know where to go next. And I've come to need a man I shouldn't have.

Turns out what I had to fear the most was the man I ran toward.

"I got involved with some bad stuff when I was a kid. Dealing on the street. Shaking down other dealers. It paid well and kept food on the table."

I nod because that's all I can do. For all the darkness I grew up in, I never knew hunger.

"I knew I didn't want that life forever, so I went into

the military." He shakes his head. "All that time and the only useful skills I have are shooting and fighting. My only local contacts were criminals. And Byron was a fucking cop. We were on opposite sides of the law, only he was the one hurting people."

I shudder. That much I knew. The upstanding cop, who rose through the ranks. Who had moved to Las Vegas and already made a name for himself. *The next police commissioner.* That's what people were saying. How honorable he was, how tough on crime. And meanwhile he was arranging deals in backrooms, setting up busts and taking the credit—and the true criminals were making bank.

And I was engaged to him. Fucking him. The brother of my sister. *Not my brother.*

"And Clara?"

He looks pensive. "For a long time I hated her. Only when I got older did I really question them leaving her behind. But I knew she had money and a family. I figured what did she need a bastard half-brother for?"

I flinch at his assessment of himself. "Kip."

He waves away my attempt at sympathy. "But then I got word she'd run, that Byron was looking for her. And you too. I knew I had to do something. I wasn't even sure what I'd do when I found her."

I remember our time in the VIP room, on the roof. In the alley. I remember every time we've been together. He started out almost sweet. Conflicted. And then he'd turned hard. He fucked me with his boot and pushed me against a brick wall. And even though it had felt good, it hadn't been kind.

"If you came for Clara, to protect her, why didn't you tell me who you were? Why did you...?"

I can't finish my question. I regret even starting it.

His expression is as grave as I've ever seen it. It feels like an apology. It feels like goodbye. "When I found you in the Grand, I realized you might have the clues to find the jewelry. That's what Byron's been looking for all this time."

My eyes fill with tears. "And you wanted to find it first."

"Maybe. Yes. Call it sibling rivalry. Call it stupidity."

"Sibling rivalry." I can't see him now. There's only tears. The dark ruddy colors of him in a wavy abstract painting. "Is that why you fucked me too? Because you knew he already had?"

Silence. That's my answer.

I close my eyes tight, squeezing a tear onto my cheek. And then another. I didn't want to cry in front of him, but it's too late. I already am. I didn't want to fall for him.

I already did. "You must have thought I was so stupid," I whisper.

"Never," he says roughly. "Brave. Strong. Beautiful. That's what you are to me."

"But you didn't help me, when you found me. Even knowing who was after me. Even knowing I didn't have a choice."

"I thought I could use you to get close to Clara but keep you at a distance. I thought I could fuck you and not care about you." His eyes are a dark sea, his anguish like waves. They batter me. They break me. "I was wrong."

It's everything I'd known and feared, that Clara is the only one worth saving.

Not me.

I don't even hate Kip in that moment. I hate myself. "I'd like to be alone," I whisper.

There is a long second where I think he might not go. Might ignore my request, like he ignored so many before. Then I hear his booted footsteps on the hardwood.

Then the quiet *click* of the door.

✧ ✧ ✧

I DON'T KNOW how much time passes. A few minutes. A few hours.

The door opens again, and my heart lurches. I don't want to see him again. But I do. I'm torn.

But it isn't Kip who walks through the door. "*Clara!*"

She runs to me, crying, and I cling to her, ignoring the pain of it, sobbing for everything—for our broken family, for Kip. For every goddamn dollar I'd picked up off the stage. We hold each other for hours, two sisters, safe together, adrift in a sea of cold men and colder women.

Clara will always be my sister.

I don't care if we have different fathers. I don't care about the color of her eyes or the alleles that would sway a DNA test. She's my sister because I kissed her fat cheeks as a baby. She would blink up at me with those blue eyes, and I think she knew who I was to her then. I was the one holding her. I was the one changing her diaper when our mother was gone.

I blame her for that—but I also know how it feels to need love.

Clara is more than my sister. I took care of her after our mother left. I never wanted her to be alone or afraid. I never wanted her to have to take care of me.

That changes today. Once I cry and hug her until my side aches, she turns the tables. "Get back in bed. You'll tear your stitches like that."

I give her my best stern look. "I'm fine."

The effect is possibly ruined by the gasp that escapes me. An arc of pain is like fire through my body.

"Bed," she repeats, her voice hard but her hands soft as she guides me under the covers.

I close my eyes as I wait for the pain and nausea to pass. When I open them again Clara is holding a glass of water and two white pills in her palm. "No," I say. "No more of that."

"The doctor said—"

"I don't care what he said. They mess with my head. I haven't been sure if I'm awake or asleep. I wasn't even sure if I was dead or alive."

Clara's eyes fill with tears. Her hand closes around

the pills as her lip trembles. "Oh, Honor."

"I'm sorry," I say, immediately contrite. I'm still not taking the pills though.

"Don't apologize," she says, sniffing. "I'm the one who left you there. I can't believe I left you. How can you forgive me?"

"There's nothing to forgive. I'm glad you left." The image of Clara tied to that bed, being beaten by a belt, is one that will never leave my head. I feel sick with it.

With a sigh, she drops the pills onto the table. They roll until one falls off the edge. The other one comes to a stop. "At least have a sip of water. You need liquids. And rest."

"I'm fine now that you're here." Not exactly fine, not with a million miles between me and Kip. I'm staying in his house, but there's more distance between us now than ever. "Speaking of which, how did you know it was safe to come back?"

"I never left. Not really. You know our neighbor on the right side?"

"The one with the mullet?"

"No, the other side. The one cooking meth on that hot plate. Anyway he came and warned me about some guys poking around. It was sweet actually."

Wait. Her expression is way too appreciative. "Please tell me you don't have a crush on Meth Guy."

She rolls her eyes. "I wasn't sure they were there for us. There are a lot of shady people in that place, you know. But I figured it would be safer to leave. I took the statue out of the window so if you came back before me you'd know it wasn't safe."

"And then you left town." That was the plan anyway, but I'm starting to have suspicions. Especially with that faintly guilty expression on her usually open face.

"Not exactly." She makes an exasperated sound. "I didn't want to leave without you, okay? Is that a crime?"

"So where did you go?" Suddenly the ceiling becomes the most interesting thing in the world to her. "Clara?"

She still won't meet my eyes. "I went looking for you, that's all."

Oh no. My eyes narrow. "Where would you possibly look for me?"

"I went to the Grand, okay?" The words are ripped from her. "I went there, and I know you're going to freak out but don't. It was fine."

Okay, somehow I survived Byron. But I'm not so sure I can make it through this. It's like there's an anvil on my head. "Are you lying to me right now? Tell me you're lying."

A sigh. "Look, you went there like every day. But I can't go there even once?"

"No," I say flatly. I want to stomp around, but that would hurt a lot. More than that, I want to wrap her in a bubble, one where creepy dudes will never stare or paw at her.

"They were actually really nice."

This only makes me more suspicious. "Who was

nice?"

"Everyone! I met Lola and Candy. They were cool once they found out I was your sister. At first they were worried about Ivan seeing me, but he said I could stay as long as I needed to."

So this is what an aneurysm feels like. Okay then. "He's a mobster, Clara. Like Dad."

She turns pensive. "Maybe that's why I felt comfortable with him. Maybe growing up like we did has made us twisted or something, like dangerous guys feel safe."

I stare at her in shock. How did she know? It had taken me forever to figure that out. And by then it was too late. I was already head over heels for a dangerous man. Already in love with his boots and his scruff and the stories he tells.

There's something around her neck. I recognize it—but not on her.

"What's that?" I ask.

She looks down, a faint smile on her lips. Her fingers grasp the marble cross I'd seen Kip wear. "He said it's for me. Something my father—my real father—left behind when he... He said I could have it."

My heart melts at the wonder in her voice. Of course she'd known she wasn't my father's daughter. And Kip must have told her the whole story. Or at least the PG-13 version. I'm glad Clara can have that sense of family now, even if it's laced with betrayal and pain. At least now she knows where she came from.

I put my hand on hers. "I'm glad." Something pricks

at me. I have faint memories from the hospital and from coming home. I must have been awake enough to talk to Clara before, but the drugs make it all seem hazy now. And something is bothering me. "How did you know to trust Kip?"

"I didn't." She gives me a rueful smile. "I gave him hell, especially when I found out he was Byron's brother."

That's my girl. "What changed your mind?"

"Well, he saved your life. Once the cops had questioned us about a hundred times, that much was clear. Even then he was demanding to see you and I was saying no. I wanted you to be fully awake and healed so you could decide for yourself if you wanted to see him."

I raise my eyebrow, a little nervous by the way she won't meet my eyes. "Something must have happened, because I have vague memories of him in my hospital room."

Her pale cheeks turn bright pink. "You kept calling for him."

"Oh." Now I think I'm blushing too, imagining crying out for him. Shouldn't I be angry at him? He lied to me. He tricked me. He also saved my life. And maybe, like Clara said, growing up like I did made me twisted or something. Maybe dangerous guys make me feel safe.

CHAPTER NINETEEN

OVER THE NEXT week I heal. And spend time with Clara. And read the book of Rudyard Kipling stories I had my sister steal from downstairs and bring to me. I even grieve for my father. He may have been twisted, but he tried to help me in the end. I believed he would have if Byron hadn't turned on him. I had the real father I'd been longing for—but only for a few seconds. That's who I mourn.

I do a lot in that week, but I don't talk much with Kip.

Or rather, he doesn't talk much to me.

I get one visit a day, and even that feels compulsory. His eyes are always shadowed, like he hasn't been sleeping. He asks me, stiffly, if there's anything I need. Like he's some kind of formal host and I'm a guest. And not his lover. Not the sister of his sister.

I don't know if we can be close again, if I can trust him again. I'm not even sure what trust is. It's all a dark miasma of lies, a twisted knot in my stomach. My mother's death. My strange sisterly relationship with Kip and with Byron. Maybe it shouldn't matter to me if we're not blood related, but if I'd known that I never would have touched Kip—not for any amount of money. And now I've touched him everywhere. He's touched me back. *Too late.*

I consider leaving the house. I'm not even sure where I'd go. Maybe it would be a relief to Kip to have me gone. Maybe he's only keeping me here out of guilt for what happened.

Or because of Clara.

What if he's disgusted by the way he saw me on that bed, naked and beaten? What if he only spent time with me because I was a stripper, because I was easy, and now that I'm lying in bed, I'm no use to him?

The next day when he comes to visit me, I'm already sitting up.

He frowns when he sees me. His eyes look haunted, but at least he's distracted enough from all that to admonish me. "You should be lying down. You're not fully recovered yet. If you push it—"

"Come sit by me," I say, patting the sheet beside me.

Normally he doesn't sit at all. One time when I asked him to, he sat on the edge of the armchair, looking so freaking uncomfortable I asked for a glass of water just so he'd have an excuse to leave. But this time I'm not going to let him off that easy.

He looks ready to refuse. God, is he actually leaner than before? Like he's not eating either...

After a long moment he nods and sits on the edge of the bed. My stomach sinks. He really does seem disgusted. "Is something wrong?" I ask softly.

He looks surprised. Then he laughs, a little rusty. "I'm not the one who got shot."

"Mhmm, but I'm making a full recovery over here. You, on the other hand…"

He shakes his head. "The last thing you need to worry about is me."

"Do you want me to leave?" My heart gives a pang as I ask the question. I don't want to leave. But I will, if he wants me to. I haven't figured out if I can live with him.

But I'm already figuring out I can't live without him.

"No! Jesus, Honor. You're way too sick to be moved."

I frown. "You make it sound like I'm dying."

"You almost did." His voice is rough. "I held you in my arms, watching you bleed out. Do you have any idea how much I—You can't leave. That's the bottom line. Don't try to fight me on this."

I hadn't wanted to leave at all. But something is still wrong. "Are you—are you grossed out by me? By how I looked when you found me?" Before he can answer, I rush to add, "Because I wouldn't be offended by that. I mean, it was awful. I hate that you saw me like that."

He looks away. A muscle in his jaw flexes. His chest rises up and down like he's forcing himself to be calm. But when he looks at me, he's anything but calm. There's fury in his eyes. "What the fuck are you talking about? *Gross?* You think I think you're *gross?*"

He's saying it like it's totally ridiculous, but I don't think it's ridiculous at all. "Well, I mean…it was pretty gross."

The marks haven't healed. I see them every time I shower, though Clara has to help me. She winces just to look at them. I'm guessing a few of the deeper ones will leave scars, but at least eventually they'll fade into some regular color instead of black-and-blue like now.

He's just staring at me now. Speechless.

I'm making a mess of this, but I'm not sure how. "Look, I don't want you to think I expect anything from you. Like a relationship or something. I know that we were just... that you were just... I know what I was," I finish lamely.

Kip stands up, tension radiating from him. He stalks to the door, and I think he must be leaving. I open my mouth to call him back, to apologize, to beg him to stay, but then he turns on his heel. Even this far away I feel his gaze sear me.

"Let me get this straight," he says. "According to you, I'm just using you for sex. I think you're gross because you were *hurt*. And I want to throw you out in the cold while you're still recovering. Does that about sum me up?"

My voice is small. "When you put it that way, it sounds kind of bad."

His eyes are like molten copper, metallic and in motion. He's panting like a bull about to charge, and suddenly my words seem like red flags.

"No, Honor," he says, taking a step forward, "I don't want you to leave. Not ever, if it's up to me."

My heart pounds. "Oh," I say, real quiet. Because *oh*.

Another step. "And when I looked at you tied to that bed, I wanted to rip apart every man that had helped put you there, every man that had hurt you. I wanted to take your wounds into my own body, feel the pain instead of you. Not once have I thought you were anything but beautiful."

I swallow hard. "Kip?"

"And as for using you for sex…" He reaches the edge of the bed, but he doesn't stop. He leans over me, one hand on either side of the headboard, his face just a foot from mine. This close his eyes are pure energy, a vortex that sucks me in and steals the air from the room. "That much is true. I want to use you for sex again and again. I never want there to come a time when I can't use you for sex, for friendship, for every goddamn thing, because I'm in love with you. Fuck, I love you."

"I love you too," I whisper. It feels almost magical, like if I talk too loud, I'll break the spell. How could he love me after everything? How could I love him? But I do.

Love doesn't ask questions. And love doesn't lie.

"No," he says, pulling back.

Um… "What?"

"You don't love me," he says flatly. "You don't even know me."

✧   ✧   ✧

NIGHT HAS FALLEN by the time I venture outside the

house. I had to wait until Clara went to sleep. Otherwise she'd worry.

It feels right to find him in the dark, where we walked holding hands, where we lay on the roof. The moon conspires with us, giving just enough light to see the lines of each other's bodies, but not enough to see all the scars.

Kip sits on the porch railing, looking at the yard with its dark morning glory blooms. He doesn't turn as I come out. He doesn't move when I walk closer. But he knows it's me. "I suppose it would be useless to order you back to bed," he says without heat.

"You could try."

He slants me a look. "Why do I get the feeling you'd enjoy that?"

"Because you know me." I lower my voice, pretending to be serious. "You know everything about me."

"Think this is a joke?"

"I'm not laughing. I'm just… You can't make these vague proclamations and expect me to just accept it. If you didn't love me—" I have to swallow past the lump in my throat. "I'd understand that. But you *do* love me, and it feels like a miracle. I can't just pretend you didn't say that to me. Unless…unless you didn't mean it."

He raises my chin with his knuckles, so I have to meet his eyes. "I meant it. Don't ever doubt that you're loved. Don't doubt I'd do anything for you."

"Then be with me," I whisper. Both in body and spirit. He's shutting me out like this, and he knows it. It hurts. It hurts more than the lashes of Byron's belt.

He swings his legs back over the balcony so he's facing me. A hand runs down my arm. "You really should be in bed. Not my bed either. You should be far away from me."

"You keep warning me away. But I know the kind of man you are. The man who wanted to help me when no one else did. The man who saved my life. And you gave up the bounty to do it—"

"Fuck the bounty," he says, harsh and loud. The word *bounty* echoes off the brick and wood of the porch. There's a lake beyond the metal fence. I see it peeking from between the trees, winking in the moonlight, beckoning. I feel suddenly tired, as if the only rest can be found underwater. I remember the poem, about the key being underground. I understand it more now, better than I could have before, how someone can want death. Not in a desperate scrabble, not violent or quick—just a slow drift to the bottom of a pond.

I look at this man in front of me, so intense, so angry. At himself?

And my sister inside, relentlessly cheerful after having lost her entire life. The father she knew. And the one who abandoned her before birth. She's lost everything.

I've failed them both, Kip and Clara. I've failed myself. I thought I was looking into the barrel of a gun before. I counted each breath as I took Clara and ran, knowing any one of them might be my last. I faced down a lunatic and got shot in the process. But none of it hurt as badly as this desolate peace.

Kip's eyes search mine, dark and knowing. "You deserve better," he murmurs.

My voice is raw when I answer. "You're all I want."

He closes his eyes. When he opens them again, I see his determination, the new openness. There are no brambles, no thorns. There is only a wide expanse, an endless earth.

"You were there," I say softly. "How?"

"I told you my father worked security for yours. I was just a kid, roaming the grounds when I wasn't allowed to. I saw you playing. You looked lonely. You looked beautiful. Even then, I think I loved you."

"When did you realize it was me?" I ask. It hurts a little that he didn't tell me. We both look different now, older, but at some point he clearly realized.

"I always knew," he says. "That's what I meant up in the room. I always knew it was you. That first night when I saw you onstage and in the private booth, I knew exactly who you were."

My stomach turns over. Maybe it shouldn't matter that he knew who I was. He could pull my hair and make me fuck his boot if I were a stranger. That would have been easier than this. Knowing what I was to him— almost family—and letting me debase myself in front of him.

"I hate what I had to do in that motel room, but I don't regret doing it. Byron has always been...off. As he got older, it got worse. Complaints from other kids.

Dead animals in the yard. We got him some counseling, and I went off to the military, too busy with not getting my ass shot to worry about what was happening back home."

"Oh, Kip."

"Then I get back to find out he's part of the fucking family now. I was fucking proud when I heard he'd become a cop, and then I find out he's as corrupt as they come. He always had a fucking thing about those jewels, thinking they were ours, that he deserved to have them." Kip runs a hand over his head. "I should have put a stop to him sooner. I should have put him down, like the fucking feral animal he'd become."

"You did," I say, feeling light-headed, like my world is crashing down around me. Like my father's stories. *Delitto d'onore.* "An honor killing."

It's one thing to think he planned to use me when I was a stranger to him. Another thing to realize he knew me all along, that he came for me and let me be afraid. I'm desperate now. Desperate enough to make excuses. I don't want to lose what we had in the bedroom. *Fuck, I love you.*

He laughs, unsteady. "So you'll pardon that too? Forget the fact that I didn't tell you who I was, forget that I didn't protect you from day one. You'll let me get away with anything, won't you?" He takes a lock of hair into his hands, rubbing it between thumb and forefinger, just like he did in the old outdoor ballroom. "My own personal martyr."

I pull back, stricken. "I know you wouldn't hurt me."

"But would I let you get hurt, Honor? We both know the answer to that. I let you work in that fucking club. I should have pulled you out the second I found you."

"Based on what? Knowing me fifteen years ago? I wouldn't have let you."

The look he gives me says I wouldn't have had a choice. "I let Byron stay with you, even though I knew he was using you. He saw it as some kind of karmic retribution for our dad leaving us. I was so relieved when I found out you'd left. Even when I found out the bounty was on your head, and I came looking for you…"

I wait, holding my breath. My heart felt heavy as a stone, sinking. Already underground. "What?"

"I thought that I could be cold with you. I wasn't the only one with a grudge. I thought I could use you to get in with your father, convince him to see Byron for what he is. And I thought I could use you to get to Clara, to make up for being absent all this time." He shakes his head. "But I saw you on that stage, and I had to wait. I told myself it was better to wait, to gain your trust. And with the side benefit that I could touch you and fuck you and sink my fingers into that soft cunt of yours."

That cunt squeezes now, muscles tight and wanting.

"I had principles, Honor. I had plans. But when I looked at you, all I could think about was keeping you with me, whatever I had to do. I threw away everything just to have you, and the only thing I regret is that you got hurt. If it weren't for that, I'd do it all over again. I'd bind you with sex and money and whatever the fuck else it took, without a single thought to what you want."

I reach down to the hem of my shirt and lift it over my head. It tugs my wound, and I wince behind the fabric, hiding it because I know he'll mind more than I do. "Then spare a thought for what I want now, Kip." My pajama pants go next, shoved down as far as I can bend and falling the rest of the way. It's far from a sexy striptease. This dimly lit porch is the opposite of a stage. But he is enthralled anyway, watching me, swallowing hard. I see the bulge in his jeans.

There won't be any lap dances tonight. I couldn't swivel my body like that if I wanted to. And maybe he's right after all. Maybe I should be in bed. But I don't care if I pull my stitches. I don't care if I hurt. It hurts worse not to be here with him, like this. Not to feel those thick fingers inside my cunt—which is ready for him. I've always been ready for him.

He slides a hand over my hip, cupping my ass. His groan is all the approval I need. What is the difference between groping and touching, between stripping and *this?* The dark heat in his eyes. The hitch in his breathing. Or maybe the way he says, "Is this okay? Am I hurting you?"

The way he cares.

"I'm fine," I breathe. I'm actually hurting, but not because he's touching me. I'm on fire, I'm burning up—

but his hand on me is cool water, soothing me. I don't ever want him to stop.

But then he does stop, when his dark gaze lands on my lingering bruises. His jaw clenches. "And you think I'm fucking sorry I killed him. The only thing I'm sorry about is not keeping him alive to do *this* to him before shooting him."

And that would only mean more pain for Kip, more guilt. "I'm glad it was quick."

"You would be," he says grimly. "You always were too forgiving."

Maybe so, but I know he'll never forgive himself. Not for letting me get hurt, not for leaving Clara as a child. Not for killing the monster that was his brother.

I will do what I can for him, though. I'll give him unconditional support, the best way I know how. All that practice stripping helps for something. I run my hands over my breasts, attracting his attention, offering myself.

He's staring at them with hunger. With need. His gaze roams lower.

And I freeze, knowing what he'll see.

I keep myself bare, usually. I shaved when I worked at the club. And before that, with Byron, I waxed. I haven't been able to do either of those things while I've been laid up recovering the past few days. There's short, stubbly hair that hasn't been trimmed or shaped at all. Self-conscious, I move to cover myself.

His hand catches my wrist. "Don't," he says gruffly.

"Don't what?"

"Don't hide from me."

I close my eyes and let my hand fall to my side. Trust. That's what this is about. He knows it, and I do too. Trust that he'll like my body when I'm no longer the smooth, sleek stripper he saw onstage. Trust that he wants me for more than sex. I don't know much about trust. It's a language I don't speak. But I hear the sound of it, the heart of it, when I'm near him. I want this badly enough to try. I need him badly enough to shake with the effort.

"Sit down," he says, gesturing to the porch swing.

I sit down on the smooth wood, feeling the slats press into my skin. Sitting straight and prim doesn't last long. With one finger under my chin, he lifts until I'm looking up—and leaning back. The bench creaks a little as I do, but I don't doubt it will hold. Even if we fuck on this, it will hold.

Like the ballroom, like the Grand, everything in this place is built to last.

"Are you afraid?" he asks. He must feel me trembling.

"Yes," I whisper.

He places a kiss on my cheek. Then lower, down my jaw. On the side of my neck. "Afraid of me?"

After a beat, I jerk my head in a nod.

He moves along my shoulder, dropping kisses while his hand slides down between my legs. "Afraid I'm like my brother?"

"You're nothing like your brother," I say on a gasp, because he's got his fingers against my pussy, rubbing gently, and it's too much. Even this light touch is too much. How will it feel when he fucks me?

Kip kneels, watching my pussy intently. With a firm hand, he pushes my legs apart. Then he leans in and places a kiss on my clit. I buck my hips into him, but then he's gone, leaving me bereft. I let out a soft whimper.

"He didn't do this?" Kip asks.

"Never."

Kip leans in and licks my pussy lips, and I shudder at the feel. I'm already strung out, tight and close to coming. Then he circles my clit with his tongue. "*Kip.*"

His eyes flash up at me. "You're going to stay very still so you don't get hurt. Just sit. Let me take care of you. Understand?"

I bite my lip. Not really an answer.

He presses two fingers inside me, and I moan. "What is it, Honor? Tell me what you're thinking. Don't hide from me."

"He never did that either," I whisper.

His fingers curl inside me, hitting a certain spot. "Did what?" he asks, voice low.

"Took care of me." I tell him what I know he needs from me, just like he gives me what I need. "You're nothing alike."

Kip doesn't respond. He just leans forward and sucks my clit, twisting his fingers—hard—and I'm thrown headlong into orgasm, unable to buck my hips or fuck his hand, unable to move at all while he wrings pleasure from my body, as he pushes me over the brink and then catches my fall, making sure I don't twist my stitches or hurt myself as I go.

"Why are you afraid of me?" he asks quietly before I can even catch my breath.

I answer him though. I wouldn't dare not to. "Because I need you."

I've always needed him. Even before I knew who he was, when I saw him in the Grand, I needed him to be real. Needed the promise of help, of relief, of safety to be real. I needed a savior. Not to get me out of danger. I ran away myself. I survived myself. I needed a savior, because I needed someone to care.

His lids lower. He looks like a big satisfied lion, licking up the cream I've spilled. He still has a bulging erection—it must be hard as steel, and painful too—but he doesn't seem to mind. No, he's far more concerned with sucking my sensitive pussy lips into his mouth, running his tongue down my slit, turning me on again when I've barely come down.

He doesn't mind that I haven't shaved or that I have scars on my body. He doesn't mind anything about me. And I understand what he means now. I don't have to hide from him. I don't have to run and hide—not ever again.

CHAPTER TWENTY

A WEEK LATER I am still reading the large book of Rudyard Kipling's stories. The old binding and yellowed pages hold the same appeal as this house, as the Grand—the same as Kip himself. Battered and beautiful.

Banging is coming from outside. Kip has been busy restoring the fascia around the house. *I've been meaning to do this for years,* he said to me. *But I never felt inspired to until you.*

They aren't the only ones battered here. I've made it through too.

Clara is not in the house. We were able to enroll her back in school once I legally got custody of her. The judge was initially suspicious of the circumstances we'd been living under. A ratty motel room and a job stripping didn't exactly inspire confidence. But it turned out he had taken bribes from Byron back when he'd been in Tanglewood. Kip privately reminded him that some scandals were best swept under the rug.

And so Byron's corruption actually helped us for once.

As I've done many times before, I flip to the beginning of the book and look at the poem inscribed there.

The jungle is a scary place for those who wander in...
Written by Kip's mother, who loved poetry. There are a few notebooks full of scribbled thoughts—a stanza here, a phrase there. There aren't many fully formed poems in verse, much less rhyme. This one is different.

The phrasing is simpler than her usual, less dense. Simpler. More childlike? The subject matter isn't childlike, though. Life and death. Being lost and never found. So why write it in a book of stories for children? In this book she'd given her son?

It holds its secrets tightly furled, locking out the wind.

It wasn't always there. I'd asked Kip about it. All the times he'd read the story as a child, this page had been blank. Only after his mother died, when he'd been paging through the book for memory's sake, had he first seen the words.

The jungle is a scary place for those who wander in...

There's something that brings me back to this poem, to this book. Like she'd left a message for Kip. Or me. As strange as it sounds, I feel like this poem is meant for me. I know how scary the jungle is. I know how it feels to wonder if death is the only way to get out.

I sigh and take a sip of my tea. Lukewarm. I've been sitting here a long time, staring. I run a finger over the ink, long dried. Her handwriting is sweetly slanted and looping. It makes me feel hopeful. From what Kip has told me about her, *she* was hopeful, despite what her husband had done, despite what Byron had become. So why write something so dire while her other son, Kip, was off fighting in the military?

I read through the poem again, lingering on the last line. *The key is underground.*

What if she had been talking about a literal key?

Everyone had thought my mother had the jewels. Or Kip's father. But what if his mother had them all along? I feel a sort of kinship with this woman I've never met, enough to guess she wouldn't have wanted to use what had come from her husband's affair. She had remained in this modest house. Would she have been able to give up the jewels entirely, though? Would she have been able to throw them away, give it away, knowing her son might benefit from it someday? I'm not sure I could have done that, thinking about what Clara could do with that money. Just like I resorted to using Byron's name with the judge to make sure Clara could stay with me. We'll do anything for the people we love, even rely on the ones we hate.

Standing up, I gather the book in my arms and run outside. "*Kip!*"

And then immediately feel contrite when I see him on a ladder. What if I'd surprised him into falling? He doesn't look surprised though, doesn't wobble at all. Instead he leans against the metal ladder as casually as if it were a wall, as if he weren't fifteen feet off the ground.

"Morning." He is wearing those boots and those jeans that I love. His legs look impossibly lean and gorgeous.

I stop and ogle him for a moment, appreciative that he is mine. He is the one onstage now.

He notices, of course. His smile is small and smug and *male.* "Need something, honey?"

He likes to call me that when he has sex on his mind. The first time he watched me closely, thinking it might offend me. Watching that closely, he could see what the word did to me instead—it got me hot. What can I say? I'm an animal when it comes down to it, and I've been trained to like that word on his tongue, to like what he does to me when he says it.

But I can't be distracted now. I hold up the book. "I need to go to the Grand."

His expression darkens. "Why?"

"I think I know what the poem is about. I think I know where she put the jewels."

WE STAND IN front of the fountain. It had been cracked before, the statue missing with only a hole where it would be. A hole that someone could drop something into. It takes construction equipment to break it apart. The stone crumbles into pieces. It will never be rebuilt.

Both Candy and Lola are there, even though the Grand won't open for another few hours. They're here to see me off. It feels like the end.

It feels like the beginning.

I hug each of them. We are friends. That is one real thing that came out of this. It's friendship born of survival and strength, of darkness and fire. We walked through that fire together. I came out alive but not unscathed. There are burns on my skin—some that are visible, like the dark red wound where the bullet went in. Some that you can't see, only feel.

Lola's lower lip is trembling, but I am the one who cries first. I am the one leaving. Even though I don't want to go back, it's still sad to say goodbye.

"Come visit me," I say. There's a part of me that wants to say *come with me. Leave this place.* But that would be a form of disrespect.

We all have our reasons for working at the Grand. Mine are gone now.

She gives me a sad smile, pulling back. "You should find different friends."

Rich friends, she means. Girls who aren't strippers or prostitutes or druggies. I squeeze her hands, keeping her with me. "I'm doing all right with the friends I have. I never got to thank you for watching out for Clara."

After a little more interrogation I had been able to rest easy. Clara hadn't seen too much that night—and Ivan had kept his hands off.

Lola brushes it off. "You don't have to thank me for that."

"I do." Then in a lower voice, I ask, "Do you think it was wrong of me to keep her hidden like that?"

Her dark eyebrows shoot up. "What? No way. You kept her alive. You kept her safe."

"Yeah." I know it's true, but there's a part of me that feels guilty anyway. Our father had kept us locked up under the guise of protection too. Maybe he meant as well as I did.

Her look is knowing. "Take it from someone who was bounced around foster homes her whole life. Being with family, no matter how much money you have or where you live."

Then I can't help it. I have to give her another hug. "Oh, Lola."

"Be proud, that's all. And get some of that." She nods towards where Kip waits for me. "You deserve happiness too."

"And you," I say softly.

"Of course." Desolation flashes through her eyes before she hides it.

I catch sight of Blue watching us. Watching *her*. His expression is unreadable, and I can't help but wonder if he wants her.

Then why hasn't he taken her?

She's stage Lola again, flirty and smooth. "Maybe I'll come visit you," she says with a wink. "We can show your boyfriend that thing we did. In the VIP room. Together."

She says that last part loud enough so Kip can hear. His expression turns both forbidding and curious, a dark look that gets me hot.

Lola, being Lola, notices and laughs. She heads back into the club. I frown when I notice Blue follow her in. Something is up with those two. I'm going to insist she really does visit me—and find out what the deal is.

Then there is Candy. She's stiff in the hug I give her.

I step back quickly, not wanting to push. "Thank—"

"It was all Lola. Trust me, if it was up to me I would've had her strung out and on the pole in two hours flat." Candy looks bored, but then again, that's how she looks whenever she's around me and Lola. She's like the inverse. She can fake interest onstage or in the lap of some asshole. But put her in front of people she actually cares about and she turns into an ice queen.

So it's interesting that she acts coldest to Ivan.

I give her a look that says I'm not buying what she's selling. She just smiles, mysterious and hard.

She's already walking away when I call out. "Did you know?"

Her face gives nothing away when she turns to look at me. "What?"

"You asked me, when you saw Kip and me together. *Does she know you're related?* Did you know about him and Byron?"

"There's not a lot that happens in this club that I don't know about."

"All seeing," I say. "Like Ivan?"

Her eyes go flat. "Nothing like Ivan."

Then she stalks off.

Then Kip calls me back, because they've reached the

bottom, the hollow beneath the fountain.

Of course we find a pile of dirt and leaves, sprinkled in by the storms. There are also cigarette butts and other unsavory items. The fountain is in front of a strip club, after all.

And we find a leather case that contains a lifetime's worth of jewels. Of treasure.

A bounty that even my father couldn't have matched.

Kip is holding the box, looking inside. I wonder what he sees. Not the dusty, vibrant jewels. His father's sin? His mother's shame?

I place a hand on his arm. "Now you can have everything your mother wanted you to."

He looks up at me, bemused. "What?"

"The mansion. The trips around the world."

He smiles. "I keep my mother's house in her memory. I've hardly lived there. I've mostly been traveling. Some for my job—private security. Others were just places I wanted to go."

"Oh."

"It's yours anyway," he says softly. "It belongs to your mother, to *you,* not me."

Yes, I could use the money. Far more than Kip, apparently, with his private security jobs and jet-setting ways. I had a few thousand stuffed under the mattress back at the motel. And my father's money, most of which was funneled into offshore accounts I didn't have access to.

Dirty money. I'm better off without it. I believe that,

but it also means I'm broke.

But I don't want to take the jewels either.

Kip doesn't see their rich colors, the shimmery strands of gold and cut jewels. And neither do I. I see my mother's wish for true love—and her betrayal when she left me behind to find it. I see my father's deepest pain when his wife left him…and the strange mercy he showed when he let her live.

These jewels belonged to my mother, but they were gifts from my father. Bought with money from booking and prostituting and shaking down other criminals. And then Kip's father stole the jewels. So who's to say who they rightfully belong to?

"Clara," I say.

Kip raises an eyebrow. "A legacy?"

"We won't tell her how they came to be here. Just that they're all that's left from our mother. And they're for her. She can buy herself a mansion or travel the world. Whatever she wants to do."

He picks up a ruby pendant, blood-red against his tanned skin. "And you? What do you want to do?"

"I wouldn't mind traveling." I look down at a crack in the sidewalk. No flower grows up between it. This isn't a place for miracles. But I'm wishing for one anyway. "Mostly I want to stay in the house with the yellow curtains and the old books."

He takes me into his arms, hands circling my waist, pulling me close. "Not much of a legacy for a mafioso's daughter."

I look into his eyes—this man of hard muscles and tattoos, of leather and chrome, of heart and honor. "We'll make our own legacy."

He brushes his lips across my cheek...my jaw...and lower. "I like the sound of that."

"That wasn't a euphemism."

"Mhmm." He's got a very hard *legacy* pressed against my stomach now, rocking gently.

"Kip, we're outside. In daylight." At least the afternoon hour means the club is closed for business. Ivan grumbled about the hassle of it all, tearing down the fountain and the money it will take to put it back to rights, but he backed down again under Kip's quiet demands. I suspect he has some dirt on Ivan actually—and isn't above using it.

Some things run in the family.

Like the fact that I'm just fine with that. This bounty rightfully belongs to my sister. And for once, finally, I know I did the right thing in running. I know she's better off in the spare room in Kip's house, going to college, and then making her way free of the ties of her past.

As for me, I have my own bounty. And that is definitely a euphemism.

His hand slides under my skirt, pushing up. Anyone passing by could see far more skin inside the club during open hours, but I'm done flashing them. Done taking my clothes off for anyone but Kip.

"The roof," I gasp as he licks and bites at the tender

skin where neck meets shoulder.

"Let's go."

He is my tiger, with his quiet way of ruling and his dark stripes, his code of honor and wildness. Beautiful and free.

THE END

Thank You

Thank you for reading Love the Way You Lie! I hope you enjoyed Kip and Honey's story...

- The next book in the Stripped series is about Blue and Lola. You can order Better When It Hurts now!

- Want to find out when my next books are available? Sign up for my newsletter at skyewarren.com/newsletter.

- Discuss this book in my Facebook group for fans: Skye Warren's Dark Room

- I appreciate your help in spreading the word, including telling a friend.

- Reviews help readers find books! Leave a review on your favorite book site.

- The Stripped series is dark, dangerous, and twisted hot. If you loved this, you will probably also love Wanderlust. Turn the page to read an excerpt from that book...

WANDERLUST

Evie always dreamed of seeing the world, but her first night at a motel turns into a nightmare. Hunter is a rugged trucker willing to do anything to keep her—including kidnapping. As they cross the country in his rig, Evie plots her escape, but she may find what she's been looking for right beside her.

"Brace yourself for an unlikely and intense love story. There are no heroes in this tale, only disturbingly beautiful monsters."

—Romantic Book Affairs

Excerpt from Wanderlust

I FELT TINY out here. Would it always be this way now that I was free? Our seclusion at home had provided more than security. An inflated sense of pride, diminishing the grand scheme of things to raise our own importance. On this deserted sidewalk in the middle of nowhere, it was clear how very insignificant I was. No one even knew I was here. No one would care.

When I rounded the corner, I saw that the lights in the gas station were off. Frowning, I tried the door, but it was locked. It seemed surreal for a moment, as if maybe it had never been open at all, as if this were all a dream.

Unease trickled through me, but then I turned and caught site of the sunset. It glowed in a symphony of colors, the purples and oranges and blues all blending together in a gorgeous tableau. There was no beauty like this in the small but smoggy city where I had come from, the skyline barely visible from the tree in our backyard. This sky didn't even look real, so vibrant, almost blinding, as if I had lived my whole life in black and white and suddenly found color.

I put my hand to my forehead, just staring in awe.

My God, was this what I'd been missing? What else

was out there, unimagined?

I considered going back for my camera but for once I didn't want to capture this on film. Part of my dependence on photography had been because I never knew when I'd get to see something again, didn't know when I'd get to go outside again. I was a miser with each image, carefully secreting them into my digital pockets. But now I had forever in the outside world. I could breathe in the colors, practically smell the vibrancy in the air.

A sort of exuberant laugh escaped me, relief and excitement at once. Feeling joyful, I glanced toward the neat row of semi-trucks to the side. Their engines were silent, the night air still. The only disturbance: a man leaned against the side of one, the wispy white smoke from his cigarette curling upward. His face was shrouded in darkness.

My smile faded. I couldn't see his expression, but some warning bell inside me set off. I sensed his alertness despite the casual stance of his body. His gaze felt hot on my skin. While I'd been watching the sunset, he'd been watching me.

When he suddenly straightened, I tensed. Where a second ago I'd felt free, now my mother's warnings came rushing back, overwhelming me. Would he come for me? Hurt me, attack me? It would only take a few minutes to run back to my room—could I beat him there? But all he did was raise his hand, waving me around the side of the building. I circled hesitantly and found another entrance, this one to a diner.

Hesitantly, I waved my thanks. After a moment, he nodded back.

"Paranoid," I chastised myself.

The diner was wrapped with metal, a retro look that was probably original. Uneven metal shutters shaded the green windows, where an OPEN sign flickered.

Inside, turquoise booths and brown tables lined the walls. A waitress behind the counter looked up from her magazine. Her hair was a dirty blonde, darker than mine, pulled into a knot. A thick layer of caked powder and red lipstick were still in place, but her eyes were bloodshot, tired.

"I heard we got a boarder," she said, nodding to me. "First one of the year."

I blinked. It was a cool April night. If I was the first one of the year, then that was a long time to go without boarders.

"What about all the trucks outside?"

"Oh, they sleep in their cabs. Those fancy new leather seats are probably more comfortable than those old mattresses filled with God-knows-what." She laughed at her own joke, revealing a straight line of grayish teeth.

I managed a brittle smile then ducked into one of the booths.

She sidled over with a notepad and pen.

"We don't usually see girls as pretty as you around here. Especially alone. You don't got nobody to look after you?"

The words were spoken in accusation, turning a compliment into a warning.

"Just passing through," I said.

She snorted. "Aren't we all? Okay, darlin', what'll it be?"

Under her flat gaze, I turned the sticky pages of the menu, ignoring the stale smells that wafted up from it. Somehow the breakfast food seemed safest. I hoped it would be easier to avoid food poisoning with pancakes than a steak.

After the waitress took my order, I waited, tapping my fingers on the vinyl tabletop to an erratic beat. I was a little nervous—jittery, although there was no reason to be. Everyone had been nice. Not exactly welcoming, but then I was a stranger. Had I expected to make friends with the first people I met?

Yes, I admitted to myself, somewhat sheepishly. I had rejected my mother's view that everyone was out to get me, but neither was everyone out to help me. I would do well to retain some of the wariness she'd instilled in me. A remote truck stop wasn't the place to meet people, to make lasting relationships. That would be later, once I had started my job. No, even later than that, when I'd saved up enough to reach Niagara Falls. Then I could relax.

When my food came, I savored the sickly sweet syrup that saturated my pancakes. It would rot my teeth, my mother would have said. Well, she wasn't here. A small rebellion, but satisfying and delicious.

The bell over the door rang, and I glanced up to see a man come in. His tan T-shirt hung loose while jeans hugged his long legs. He was large, strong—and otherwise unremarkable. He might have come from any one of those eighteen-wheelers out there, but somehow I knew he'd been the one watching me.

His face had been in the shadows then, but now I could see he had a square jaw darkened with stubble and lips quirked up at the side. Even those strong features paled against the bright intensity of his eyes, both tragic and terrifying. So brown and deep that I could fall into them. The scary part was the way he stared—insolently. Possessively, as if he had a right to look at me, straight in my eyes and down my neckline to peruse my body.

I suddenly felt uncomfortable in this dress, as if it exposed too much. I wished I hadn't changed clothes. More disturbing, I wished I had listened to my mother. I looked back down at my pancakes, but my stomach felt stretched full, clenched tight around the sticky mass I'd already eaten.

I wanted to get up and leave, but the waitress wasn't here and I had to pay the bill. More than that, it would be silly to run away just because a man looked at me. That was exactly what my mom would do.

Back when we still left the house, someone would just glance at her sideways in the grocery store. Then we'd flee to the car where she'd do breathing exercises before she could drive us home. I was trying to escape that. I *had* escaped that. I wouldn't go back now just because a man with pretty eyes checked me out.

Still, it was unnerving. When I peeked at him from beneath my lashes, I met his steady gaze. He'd seated himself so he had a direct line of vision to me. Shouldn't he be more circumspect? But then, I wouldn't know what was normal. I was clueless when it came to public interaction. So I bowed my head and poked at the soggy pancakes.

Once the waitress gave me the bill, I'd leave. Simple enough. Easy, for someone who wasn't paranoid or crazy. And I wasn't—that was my mother, not me. I could do this.

When the waitress came out, she went straight to his table. I drew little circles in the brown syrup just to keep my eyes off them. I couldn't hear their conversation, but I assumed he was ordering his meal.

Finally, the waitress approached my table, wearing a more reserved expression than she had before. Almost cautious. I didn't fully understand it, but I felt a flutter of nerves in my full stomach.

She paused as if thinking of the right words. Or maybe wishing she didn't have to say them. "The man over there has paid for your meal. He'd like to join you."

I blinked, not really understanding. The gentleness of her voice unnerved me. More than guilt—pity.

"I'm sorry." I fumbled with the words. "I've already eaten. I'm done."

"You have food left on your plate. Doesn't matter how much you want to eat anyway." She paused and then carefully strung each word along the sentence. "He requests the pleasure of your company."

My heart sped up, the first stirrings of fear.

I supposed I should feel flattered, and I did in a way. He was a handsome man, and he'd noticed me. Of course, I was the only woman around besides the waitress, so it wasn't a huge accomplishment. But I wasn't prepared for fielding this kind of request. Was this a common thing, to pay for another woman's meal?

It was a given that I should say no. Whatever he wanted from me, I couldn't give him, so it was only a question of letting him down nicely.

"Please tell him thank you for the offer. I appreciate it, I do. But you see, I really am finished with my meal and pretty tired, so I'm afraid it won't be possible for him to join me. Or to pay for my meal. In fact, I'd like the check, please."

Her lips firmed. Little lines appeared between her brows, and with a sinking feeling I recognized something else: fear.

"Look, I know you aren't from around here, but that there is Hunter Bryant." When I didn't react to the name, her frown deepened. "Here's a little advice from one woman to another. There are some men you just don't say no to. Didn't your mama ever warn you about men like that?"

Want to read more? Wanderlust is available at Amazon.com, BarnesAndNoble.com, and iBooks.

Other Books by Skye Warren

Standalone Dark Romance

Wanderlust

On the Way Home

His for Christmas

Hear Me

Stripped Series

Tough Love (prequel)

Love the Way You Lie

Better When It Hurts

Pretty When She Cries

Criminals and Captives Series

Prisoner

Dark Nights Series

Trust in Me

Don't Let Go

ABOUT THE AUTHOR

Skye Warren is the New York Times and USA Today Bestselling author of dark romance. Her books are raw, sexual and perversely romantic.

Sign up for Skye's newsletter:
www.skyewarren.com/newsletter

Like Skye Warren on Facebook:
facebook.com/skyewarren

Join Skye Warren's Dark Room reader group:
skyewarren.com/darkroom

Follow Skye Warren on Twitter:
twitter.com/skye_warren

Visit Skye's website for her current booklist:
www.skyewarren.com

ACKNOWLEDGEMENTS

Thank you to Shari Slade, Annika Martin, Leila DeSint, and Lina Sacher for your insights. Thank you also to beta readers Liz, Arc, Tiffanie, and Trish.

Many thanks to Leanne Schafer and Sharon Muha for your careful editing.

Thank you to Neda at the SubClub books for your work on the release. Plus Giselle at Xpresso Book Tours, Nicole at Indie Sage, and Debra at The Book Enthusiast for your help too. And thank you to all the bloggers who shared my cover reveal and new release.

Thank you to Sara Eirew for the gorgeous photo. So pretty!

Thank you to Paul at BB eBooks for his fabulous formatting, as always.

And last but not least, thank you to my readers, my Dark Room members, my Facebook fans, my twitter followers, my newsletter subscribers, and every reader who came out to support me in this release.

COPYRIGHT

Love the Way You Lie © 2014 by Skye Warren
Print Edition

Cover design by Book Beautiful
Cover photograph by Sara Eirew
Formatting by BB eBooks

Made in the USA
Lexington, KY
14 January 2017